Telling Tales

Susan Price

Hodder
Children's
Books

a division of Hodder Headline plc

A Catalogue record for this book is available
from the British Library

ISBN 0 340 70903 0

Typeset by Avon Dataset Ltd, Bidford-on-Avon, Warks

Printed and bound in Great Britain by
The Guernsey Press Co. Ltd, Channel Islands

Hodder Children's Books
A division of Hodder Headline plc
338 Euston Road
London NW1 3BH

Contents

One

The Bride's New Clothes

'Now who'll tell us a story?'

The fire shone bright on the colours of the rag-rug before the hearth, while its warmth, and scent of burning heather filled the room. Lamp-light ran in shimmers along the blades of clacking scissors, and needles glinted as they stabbed in and out. Huge shadows of ducked heads and flying arms were thrown onto the far wall.

'A story, come on, a story!'

Marie was to marry, and they had all gathered to stitch the sheets and pillow-cases, the shifts and skirts, the towels and bonnets and table-cloths she would need as a wife. Sheets were shaken, the draught making the fire burn brighter and the smell of burning mingled with that of freshly laundered linen.

Brilliant pink ribbon, to be threaded through the edges of caps and bodices, shone with a satiny sheen. A tangle of embroidery silks, green, blue, yellow, red, tumbled across the cream of a nightshirt.

'Granny Shearing, are you going to tell the story?'

1

'No,' said Granny, and Snap! went her big scissors.

'Letty, you'll tell us one?'

But Letty was busy measuring from the bride's waist to her feet. 'Not now, not now.'

'Somebody's got to tell we a story. Clo, will *you*?'

Clo, a pretty young woman, stooped over a little loom she held in her lap. On it she deftly wove a narrow strip of brightly-coloured and patterned braid, to decorate the hems, cuffs and necks of the bride's new clothes. 'I'll tell one,' she said.

'Ssh!'

'Clo's going to tell a story!'

'Listen!'

'Ssh!'

'It happened once,' said Clo, 'that there was a farmer who loved his wife, loved her deep and dear, and when her was to have his babby, there was nothing in this world could make him happier. But the woman had hard time of it. The babby was born alive. The mother died.'

'Oh Clo, you could tell happier story!'

'Ssh!'

'Listen!'

'Go on, Clo.'

'Farmer was so miserable, he wouldn't even look at the babby. When midwife brought it to him, he says, "Take it away. Let it follow its mother. I've no use for it." And he shut hisself up in his house and wouldn't listen to nothing anybody said to him, not to the midwife, not to the vicar, not to the doctor, not to nobody.

'Midwife took babby home with her and looked after it, but every day her walked over to farm, and knocked on doors and windows and shouted, "What's he to be christened? Come on, he's got to have a name, what's he to be called?"

'Farmer sticks his head out of upstairs window, and says, "Call him Tristan."

' "That's an unlucky name to give a tiny little babby," says midwife – 'cause Tristan means "Born For Sorrow" – "That's like a curse," her says.

' "I don't care," says farmer. "He was born in sorrow and he's born for sorrow, and that's his name."

'So midwife had the babby christened Tristan, and goes on looking after him, even though her was a widow on her own and had hardly any money. "But somebody's got to look after him," her says. "Nobody else is going to do it, so I shall." The neighbours used to help her out when they could – and then, for shame, the farmer started giving her some money every week, to pay for his son's keep. But he would never so much as look at the little boy, let alone pick him up or talk to him. So when Tristan started growing up, and calling the midwife "Mummy", her had to tell him that her wasn't his mummy, that he didn't have a mummy, though he did have a daddy. Her pointed out Tristan's daddy as the farmer went past midwife's little house.

' "Why don't I live with him, like other boys live with their daddies?" says Tristan.

3

' " 'Cause he named you Tristan," says midwife. " 'Cause he doesn't want you."

'Then a visitor come calling at midwife's house, asking for Tristan. "My name's Mark Cornwall," he says. "I'm Tristan's mother's brother." He lived a long way off, in another county, so it had taken a long time for the gossip to reach him, but in the end, he'd heard about how his sister had died, and her babby was being looked after by strangers.

' "I can't be doing with that," he says. "I'll take the little lad home with me and bring him up like my sister would have wanted."

' "And what's his dad got to say to that?" midwife asks. "I can't just go handing him over to you."

' "I've been and spoken with his father," says Farmer Cornwall. "He don't care where the poor little beggar goes, so long as he don't have to see him. Don't you think he'd be better where he's wanted?"

' "He's wanted here," says midwife. "I've looked after him since he was born, he's like my own child."

' "Then come with we," says Farmer Cornwall. "I'm not married, so I've nobody at home to look after him. I daresay the nipper would be happier if you come along, and it'd save me hiring a nursemaid."

' "Well, I don't know," says midwife. "I should miss me house and neighbours . . . But then, I should miss Tris more. I've talked meself into it – I shall come."

'So Tristan growed up on his uncle Mark's farm, and he was happy. Seemed he'd been named all wrong. Him and

Farmer Cornwall took to each other like bread and cheese, and Farmer soon started taking the boy about with him, so he could learn all the business of the farm. Tristan was a bright lad. Tell him something once and he knowed it – and he worked out a whole lot more for hisself. Farmer Cornwall soon gives him a little calf and a little pig to look after, and lets him keep the money from 'em. Farmer was always boasting about what a clever lad Tristan was. "Looks just like his dead mother," he'd say, "and a stockman already and he ain't up to me belt buckle yet! I did a good day's work when I fetched him home."

'But when Tristan was sixteen, the midwife died. Her'd always been a mother to him, and for a long time Tristan was as sad as his name. Farmer Cornwall was sad an all – he'd been fond of the old woman. All his mates down the pub says, "Why did you and the old biddy never get hitched?"

' "Ah, we was never the lovey-dovey marrying types, me and the old girl," says Farmer.

' "You ought to find yourself some little body and wed her now," say his mates. "Somebody to keep house and cook for you and the lad."

' "Me and Tris can manage fine," says Farmer. "We don't need nobody."

' "Tris is a good lad," they says, "but he ain't your own. You ought to get some little uns of your own, somebody to leave all that good land to."

' "Tris'll get the land when I go," says Farmer. "He's earned it. Stop going on about marrying. I've never fancied wedlock and I ain't starting courting at my time of life."

'But the talk must have put an idea into his head. It was spring. Martins was nesting in the eaves of the farmhouse, flying backwards and forwards with sticks and straws and bits of wool and hair to make their nests. Farmer Cornwall stepped out of his door one day, and felt something touch his face with a light, light touch. He puts up his hand and caught a hair that a martin had dropped. He stretches it out between his fingers, and it was a long, long hair – a woman's hair – and it shone bright red and gold – redder than leaves at the turn of the year, more gold than a gold sovereign.

'Just then Tristan steps out the door behind him, and Farmer shows him the hair and says, "I wonder whose head that come from?"

' "Oh, I can tell you," says Tristan. "Only one woman with hair that long, that fine and that red. Soldy Ireland from over Romney way."

'Next thing is, Farmer Cornwall starts asking around, and he finds that Soldy Ireland's the daughter of another farmer. So, next Sunday, instead of going to his own church, he goes over to the one at Romney. "I feel like a change," he says. In church he gets a look at Soldy, and her's beautiful. Outside in the churchyard, he sees her pull off her hat, and down falls all her long, red hair. And Farmer Cornwall starts thinking it wouldn't be such a bad idea to have a little wife all to hisself, to cook and clean and warm his bed, and look pretty on his arm as they walk to church. So Farmer Cornwall goes over to see Farmer Ireland, and they talk, and decide it'd be a good thing for Farmer Cornwall to marry Soldy. Them was the days when a girl was told who her'd marry, and no argument.

'Well, Tristan felt a bit slapped in the face when his uncle told him he was wedding Soldy Ireland – but then he thinks, if the girl's willing, why shouldn't the old man have a bit of happiness? So he congratulates his uncle and wishes him all the best.

'Down the pub, though, Tristan's mates say, "Now the old man'll have ten brats, one after the other, and they'll get everything when he pops his clogs. You'll be left with nothing but the worn-out old shirt on your back – after all the hard work you've put in an' all." Tristan tells 'em to mind their own business. He knows his uncle Mark wouldn't do him down like that.

'Anyroad, over at Romney, Soldy Ireland ain't happy at all. Her don't want to wed Farmer Cornwall. "He's old," her says. "He's fat."

' "Listen, I know it all looks bad now," says her mother, "but it'll work out. Remember, he's an old man and you'll still be a young woman when he dies, and a rich widow to boot. You'll be able to please yourself who you marry then – or live your own life with money to throw at the birds."

' "But that might be years away!" says Soldy.

' "They'll be happy years," says her mother. "Don't worry. I shall make you up one of my special drinks for you and Farmer Cornwall to share on your wedding night."

' 'Cause Mrs Ireland, Soldy's mother, knowed a sight more than her prayers. The drink her mixed up, with lots of honey and ginger, was a love-philtre. Her meant to make sure that her daughter was happy.

'So Farmer Cornwall and Soldy went to church together and made their vows afore the altar – and Tristan was best man. And then they went back to the farmhouse for the wedding feast, with all their relatives and neighbours, and at the end of the feast, the neighbours undress the couple and put 'em to bed, and in comes Soldy's mother with her special drink in a big cup. Her watched to make sure that Soldy drunk half and Farmer Cornwall drunk half. And then her went home with the other neighbours and left 'em to it.

'Ooh!' said the women round the fire. 'Ooh, Marie!'

'Her don't know what you're talking about!'

'Her knows. I seen her with the lads in Milking Bank Lane.'

'Is that a blush, Marie?'

Clo went on weaving her braid until Marie said, 'Go on, Clo. Don't mind about this lot. What happened next?'

'Honey and ginger ain't everything,' Clo said. 'Soldy pinned up her hair, like a proper married woman, and tucked it all away under a cap, but her was a lovely girl for all that, and her hair kept slipping down from under the cap. And Tristan was a good-looking, well set-up young chap, and every morning they et breakfast together in the kitchen, and every evening they et dinner together, and sat by the same fire. Every day they met each other round the farm. Tristan hadn't had so much as a sip of the love-philtre, but he was soon as lovesick as if he'd knocked back a gallon of it. While he was in the same room as Soldy, he was all the time peeking at her, and then looking away fast when her looked at him. He started to bungle his work, because his head was all the time full of Soldy, and what her might be doing, and how things might have been if his uncle hadn't married her first. At night he couldn't sleep for thinking about her, and by day he couldn't eat because it was Soldy who'd packed up the bread and cheese he ate in the field, and Soldy who put the plate in front of him at the kitchen table.

'And, o'course, he couldn't do anything about it, 'cause Soldy was his uncle's wife, and his uncle had taken him in and given him a proper home, not just clothing him and feeding him, but loving him as well. And anybody, even a stranger, would see in a minute that the old man doted on his Soldy.

'Things got so bad for Tristan that he thought he'd have to leave and find paid work in some other part of the country, 'cause he couldn't bear to see his uncle stroking Soldy's hair and patting her bum and going up the stairs with her every night. He catched sight of his reflection in the farm's pond, and says to it, "This is the sorrow I was born for!" His father's curse had catched him up.

'And Soldy . . . Soldy loved her husband, and maybe that was just 'cause of her mother's magic drink, and maybe it wasn't. The old man was always gentle with her, always patient and kind, and her come to love him 'cause he loved her so much . . . but her was young and curious, and couldn't help looking sideways at Tristan and wondering what it would be like with him. And her seen Tristan watching her, and looking away when her looked at him; and how he hung about the kitchen as long as he could when her was there. Her noticed how quick he was to lift things for her, and carry things for her, but yet couldn't find a word to say for hisself when her was in the same room.

'But he never so much as blowed her a kiss, and her knowed he never would so long as her was married to his uncle. That made things hard . . . In the end, her slipped out into the yard after Tristan one night, when he went to check on the animals, and her waited for him in a dark corner back of the outhouse, and when he come up, her just put her arms round him and hugged him. That was enough. He put his arms round her and kissed her, and her kissed him – but somebody else come out into the yard, and they had to stop, and go back into the kitchen afore they was missed, trying to pretend that they hadn't been up to anything.

'And after that . . .'

'Where there's a will, there's a way,' said Granny Shearing, snipping through some overlong threads.

'Oh, that's so,' said Clo. 'Soldy would sneak out to where Tristan was working. Tristan would sneak back to the house in the morning or the afternoon. Both of 'em would sneak out into the yard in the evening. Every time they thought they'd be copped. There was so many folk about, coming and going, it didn't seem they could keep on getting away with it – but, o'course, old Farmer Cornwall was so trusting. He liked to see his Soldy and his Tris getting on together. He never would have believed that his sweet darling little wife, or Tris, who was like his son, would do anything to hurt him.

'Soldy and Tristan knowed that an' all. And they knowed they was going to hurt him, sooner or later. A dozen times one or the other of 'em said, "We must never do this again." And the other one would agree. And Tristan would make more plans to leave home, and Soldy would say, "That'd be best." But Tristan never went anywhere – he couldn't have done it – and Soldy wouldn't have let him go – and within a week they was sneaking round to meet each other again.

'One afternoon old Cornwall needed Tristan for something, and he hunted all round the farm for him, in every field, behind every hedge, in every outbuilding – until, in the end, there was only one place left to look for him, and that was back at the farmhouse. So old Cornwall goes swinging up the farmhouse's narrow stairs and barged into the little cubby-hole that Tristan slept in, shouting, "What you doing back at the house in the afternoon, have you got a bellyache?"

'And there's Tristan all right. On his bed. With sweet darling little Soldy. The pair of 'em without a stitch of clothing between 'em, and curled up together closer than the lid is to the eye.

'Old Cornwall saw 'em; and then he steps out of the room, stands on the landing and thinks about it; and then he goes down into the kitchen and leans on the wall and takes a lot of deep breaths. He's telling hisself that he hadn't seen what he'd seen – or who he'd seen. It was somebody else, just a couple of the farm-servants. Or Tristan had been taken ill, and Soldy was just trying one of her mother's cures on him . . .

'Oh aye, I've tried that cure meself,' said Letty. 'It'll cure a lot of ills, that cure.'

'But he knows what he's seen,' said Clo. 'Back up the stairs he goes.

'In the little room Tristan and Soldy, all scared, are pulling on their clothes fast as they can. "Aye, get dressed!" shouts old Cornwall. "You'll need to get dressed, 'cause you're out the door, you, you backbiting back-stabber," he says to Tristan. "Out of my sight afore I kill you – But, oh, not you, Madam!" And he grabs Soldy's arm as her tries to get past him. "You'm not going anywhere. You'm going to stand up in front of the altar and let everybody see what a dirty bag you are. I'll see you in the stocks for this, you little basket."

'What an uproar! Soldy's fighting to get loose, sobbing and screaming; and Tristan's shouting, and he comes and tries to make the old man let her go. So the old man hits him, and Tristan don't hit back at first, 'cause he feels bad about it all, but the old man keeps thumping him so he has to fend him off, and Soldy's screeching worse than ever and trying to pull 'em apart. There's such a row going on, such a stamping of feet and shoving against walls, that the servants come up from the kitchen – they thought murder was being done – and they get hold of 'em all, and bundle 'em downstairs.

'The row carries on in the kitchen. Old man Cornwall's calling his wife and nephew filthy names, and Tristan and

Soldy are trying to explain and shouting that they're sorry, and other folks are saying how they *knowed* something was going on. Some folk was trying to calm things down, and others was trying to stir things up, and everybody was taking sides. Tristan sees there's nothing to be done – his uncle will never listen – and he just catches hold of Soldy's hand and runs out of the kitchen into the yard, dragging her behind him. They run off across the yard and into the dark fields afore most folk know what's going on, let alone afore anybody can stop 'em.

'Old man Cornwall stands in the doorway and yells after 'em, "Run! Sleep in the rain! Starve! Freeze! Serve you right! See if I care!"

'But care he did, and next morning he was out early, with all his men, looking for 'em. When he found 'em, he said, he was going to have 'em both shamed at church, and he'd send Soldy back to her parents in disgrace, neither wife nor maid – and he'd see to it that Tristan wouldn't find hiding nor lodging in the whole county. Then he'd shake his head and say, "But it was a cold night last night, it was a cold night to sleep out."

'It was a cold night, and Soldy and Tristan never sat down nor lay down, but kept tramping on, to stay warm. They didn't get far – just went round and round in a circle, 'cause they got a bit lost in the dark, and couldn't think what to do or where to go anyroad. "We'll have to go back, no matter how bad it is," Soldy says. "I'll go to my mother."

' "You'll be in trouble," Tristan says. "We'll go away,

where nobody can find us and nobody knows us."

' "We haven't got any clothes or any money," says Soldy. "What will we live on? How will we eat?"

' "Better to beg and sleep under hedges than go back to what we'd be going back to," says Tristan. "We'll cross the county border," he says, "and get to a town. There'll be hundreds of people there and nobody'll know us or notice us." And as soon as it's light, they set off for the border.

'They tramp all day, and they're cold and wet, and aching all over, and tired out and hungry. There was houses where they could have asked for shelter and food, but they was still too close to home, and they was ashamed to go where they might be knowed.

'The second night they couldn't sleep for cold and damp and hunger, but they rested in the corner of a field, under a dripping hedge, cuddling up together to try and find some comfort. "I'm sorry," Tristan kept saying. "I'm sorry."

' "T'aint your fault," Soldy says. "I'm as much to blame."

'By the time light come they was in a bad way, but they struggled on, and when they come to a farm, they went up to the door and knocked and asked for something to eat. The farm-wife took one look at them and said, "Come in and sit by the fire, the both of you." She give 'em towels, and mugs of hot tea, and a bowl of porridge each.

'Tristan asked her where they was, and she told 'em, and then they knowed that they was just over the border into the next county, so they might be far enough away to be safe from Old Cornwall.

14

' "And what are you doing, wandering about?" says the farm-wife. "You neither of you look like tramps to me."

'Tristan told her they was running away from Soldy's dad and his uncle, who wouldn't let 'em be together.

'There's a nice bending of the truth into a lie,' said Granny Shearing.

'The farm-wife felt proper sorry for 'em then, and asked what they could do. Well, 'course, Soldy could bake and brew and weave and spin, and Tristan could do all sorts of farm-work. "You stay here until I speak to my husband," said the farm-wife. "We might have work for you; and there's always plenty of food round here, and you can crawl into a warm corner somewhere."

'The farmer had nothing against it, so they stopped at the farm for a bit – just while they drew breath and looked round for something better – but maybe they should have gone on, because old Cornwall gets to hear of 'em, don't he? And the next thing is, he turns up, with a gang of his farm-men. He barges his way into the farm's kitchen, grabs Soldy by her arm and her hair, and tries to drag her outside. Her starts yelling, and the farm-wife joined in, as well as hitting old Cornwall with a ladle and anything else her could get her hands on.

'Tristan and the farmer, and other farm-men come running, and there was scuffling and bawling and pushing and thumping. Then the two sides fell back a bit and panted and talked.

' "That's my wife, my legal wife," says old Cornwall,

pointing at Soldy. "I'm taking her back with me."

' "Her's my wife," says Tristan, "and her's staying."

'The farmer's got a good idea who's telling the truth, but he's taken a dislike to old Cornwall. "I don't know whose wife her is," he says, "and I'm not seeing any young wench dragged off my land by a bunch of bruisers I don't know from Adam."

' "And I'm not leaving without my wife," says old Cornwall. "I'm staying right here."

'So then the farm-wife speaks up. "This needs to be settled once and for all," her says. "The King's court's not far from here, and the flag's flying, so the King's in residence. Go and put your case to the King, and let him settle it. What other use is he?"

'It was decided then, that they'd go to the King's court, and abide by whatever settlement the King made. So off they go in a troop: Old Cornwall and all his men, and the farmer and all *his* men, to make sure Tristan and Soldy was all right; and the farm-wife who went along out of curiosity, and a lot of other nosey parkers who tagged along an' all.

'It was a good job the farm-wife took along a lot of food 'cause once they got to the castle, they had to wait two days afore the King could see 'em. He had lots of other people to see. But they was able to sleep warm and dry in the castle's hall.

'Then come the day when their case was heard. Clerks talked to 'em first, to find out what it was all about. Then they was took into the great hall, and there, at the end, was the big chair, and King Arthur sitting in it, with his guards on either side of him.

'The clerks told the King what the case was all about. Here was Mark Cornwall, a farmer, who'd come to claim back his wife, this woman, Soldy Cornwall, who had run away with his nephew, this young man Tristan, who'd seduced the wife away.

' "Why am I troubled with so footling a case?" says the King. "Let the old man bring witnesses to attest that he is the lawful husband and, that done, let him take the woman away and punish her how he will. Then let the seducer be whipped."

' "Oh no, King!" says old Cornwall.

' "You have something to say?" says the King.

' "King, I was angry when this first happened," says old Cornwall. "I wanted my wife shamed outside church, I wanted my nephew whipped and turned out . . . But now I've cooled down and . . . Well, they're both young. These things happen. If I can take my wife home with me, I'm willing to let it rest at that. Let the lad go free to find his own living where he can. He don't need whipping an' all."

'The King's thinking this over, when Tristan says, "King, may I speak?" The King nods. "King," Tristan says, "I'm not Soldy's husband by law, but I am by right. Her never wanted to marry my uncle. He's a good man, but he's old and not to her fancy. He loves her, but her never loved him like her loves me – and I love her the same! If her'd been married to me, her never would have left me for anybody else." And

Soldy stands by him, nodding her head hard.

' "I married her!" says old Cornwall. "I had her mother and father's good will. I paid a dowry for her! I made me vows in church, afore the altar, and her made hers! So that's that."

' "Her didn't know me when her married him," says Tristan. "Her was just being a good girl and doing what her mam and dad wanted her to do, not knowing any better. So what if her mam and dad wanted it? It ain't their wedding! So what if a dowry was paid? Is it all money and laws? Her *wants* to be with me and her don't want to be with him. Don't that count for nothing?"

' "Hmm," says King Arthur. "This is a more difficult case than I thought." All his clerks step forward to give him advice, but he waves 'em away. "I shall retire and think about it," he says, "and give my judgement tomorrow."

'So they had another day to hang about the castle. Tristan and Soldy stayed with the farm-wife, her husband and their people, and Old Cornwall stayed with his people, and neither side talked to the other. It wasn't a happy time.

'Next day, they all goes back into the great hall to hear King Arthur give his judgement.

' "Here's my decision," says the King. "Cornwall has a husband's rights by law and custom, and that cannot be lightly overthrown. But Tristan has a husband's rights by way of nature and the woman's own inclining – nor can that be lightly set aside. So it is my decree that the two men shall share the woman. One shall have her while the leaves are on the trees, and the other while the leaves are off the trees. The husband to choose, by right of seniority and legal right."

' "But—" says Cornwall.

' "But—" says Tristan.

' "That is our decision, the decision of your King," says King Arthur. "There is to be no argument. Now, old man, choose."

' "Well . . ." says Cornwall, and he's thinking hard. "Well then, I choose to have her while the leaves are off the trees, 'cause that's when the nights are longest."

'And Soldy sang out, "Oh praise be, praise be, to King Arthur and the red-berried yew, to King Arthur and the green-needled pine, to Arthur and the ever-green holly, for as long as the yew, the pine and the holly have leaves, I shall be with Tristan."

' "But—" old Cornwall starts to say. "That's. I. If."

' "Quiet," says King Arthur. "We've been outwitted, you and I. It's best we keep our tongues still, and accept the judgement of the yew, the pine and the holly." And from his finger he took a gold ring and give it to Soldy, so her and Tristan had something to start their new life with.

'And that's the end of my story. If you want any more, you must tell them yourselves.'

There was a sighing round the fire, and murmurs of, 'Oh, good story,' and, 'I'm glad it ended like that.' And then a little more sewing was done in silence, and home-made wine and scones were handed round. And then,

'We've had a story from Clo. Who'll tell us another? Granny, will you?'

'Not yet,' says Granny, snapping her scissors through a length of ribbon. 'It's too early in the night.'

'I will,' says Letty, rolling up her tape-measure and sitting down. 'So let's have some hush now. Listen.

'This is a true story I'll tell you, with never a word of a lie.

'There was this cobbler, and he had a wife, and he never used his hammer to hammer a nail into a boot harder than he used his fist to hammer her.

'He was a bad lot. He'd take his money to the pub and get plastered, and then he'd take out the money he needed for leather and twine and nails, and what was left he'd give to her for housekeeping – but he expected to eat like a king on that! If he didn't like what her served him up for dinner, her'd get the plate in her face, and then a kicking and a punching. It was the same if his dinner wasn't on the table when he walked through the door – or if he thought it had been on the table waiting for too long and had got cold. The poor woman couldn't do anything right.

'Her got thumped for looking a mess – he didn't want to be married to a fright and a frump. Not that her had much chance to look anything else, poor woman, with her old clothes and her bruised face. If her did try to look smart, then he said, "Who you think you're doing yourself up for?" and thumped her again.

'He said the house was a tip and he was ashamed to bring anybody home, and anyroad, he couldn't ask his friends to eat the pig swill her served up. Her was ugly, he said, and her stunk, and her was a drag on him. He could never get on in life and make something of hisself while her was dragging him down. If her tried to stand up for herself or answer back, he'd punch her, and lay his belt across her back.

' "I'm stuck with you," he said. "Till death us do part.' Why I ever wed you, I don't know. Biggest mistake of my life."

' "Biggest mistake of mine," her said, once, and got the worst beating he'd ever given her. Her couldn't hardly lift her hand after it.

'Anyroad, there come a market-day, and all the pubs was open for it, and the cobbler spent the morning getting drunk and complaining about his wife, and how he'd be a rich man if it wasn't for her wasting his money. "I wish I was rid on her," he says.

' "Well, why don't you get rid on her?" somebody says. "It's market-day. Sell her."

' "I shall!" he says, being drunk. And he bought a length of rope, and home he went, and put the rope round his wife's neck. Her knowed better than to ask any questions, and her let him lead her off, all through the streets to the market-place, with this rope round her neck.

'And in the market-place, he makes her stand on the steps of the market-cross, where everybody can see her, and he starts bawling, "Wife for sale! Come buy, come buy! Who wants a wife? Wife for sale, going cheap!"

'A crowd soon gathers, all laughing.

' "How much?"

' "Five shilling!" says the cobbler.

'The crowd jeers. "Too much, too much! Five shilling for a skinny stick like her? Never!"

' "What's her cooking like?"

' "How is her at making the bed?"

'Now there happened to be a shepherd in the crowd, watching. He had a space all to hisself 'cause, being a shepherd, he stunk of sheep. And he wasn't used to towns and crowds, and he didn't like all this jeering and shouting. He seen this poor woman standing there, her shoulders all hunched and trying to hide her face. But every time her husband pulled on the rope and jerked up her head, he catched sight of the bruises. And the shepherd calls out, "I'll give you a shilling!"

'Everybody in the crowd turns to look at the shepherd and they're all laughing. "You got a bid!"

' "Going, going—"

'Somebody else, just for the fun of it, calls out, "One and a tanner!"

' "Two shilling!" says the shepherd.

'The cobbler starts winding up the rope. "I want five shilling."

'Men started climbing up the steps of the market-cross. "Hey, hey, you've got to take the bid."

' "You put her up for sale – he's bid."

'One man turned to the crowd. "I'm bid two shilling. Anything more than two shilling?"

'Folk was all looking at the shepherd. They wanted to see him win the bid now.

' "I'll give you two and six," the shepherd says.

'Folk am pulling at the cobbler's arm. "That's half what you wanted. Come on. Complete the sale." And they're waving to the shepherd to come up. "Let's see your money."

'The shepherd goes up the cross steps, and shows the money in his hand. The rope was taken out of the cobbler's hand and put into the shepherd's. "Take your money," folk said to the cobbler. To the shepherd, they said, "Take your wife."

'The shepherd took the rope from round the woman's neck, and takes her hand and leads her down the steps – and her went with him. Folk cheered as they went away down the street.

'Well, the woman and the shepherd walked all the length of the street without looking at each other. Then the shepherd stopped and he says – still not looking her in the face – "Listen, I'm sorry. I just wanted to stop all that. You can go now if you want to. Or if you've got a mother or a sister or somebody to go to, I'll walk you there."

' "What about your money?" the woman says. And her's looking at him, and he's nothing special. Brown and wrinkled from being out in all weathers. Bald.

' "Oh, never mind the money," he said. "I'll manage."

' "Have you got a wife?" her said.

' "No," he said. "I've never had a wife. I'm not around folk that often."

' "Could you do with a wife?" her said. "To cook and clean? And that?"

23

'He says, "I. Well. I dunno. Maybe. I manage."

' "You spent your money on a wife," her said. "And I'm well rid of that sod back there, I can tell you. So let's see how we do manage."

'So the woman went back with the shepherd, to the little house in the hills where he lived, all on his own and miles from anywhere. It was a tidy enough place, because the shepherd wasn't in it enough to make it untidy, but it wasn't very comfortable, and it was a bit dusty.

' "You have the bed," the shepherd says. "I'll sleep on the hearth."

' "I won't turn you out of your bed," her says.

' "I can't let you sleep on the hearth," he says.

' "I don't mean to sleep on the hearth," her says. "I mean to sleep in the bed with you. I'm your wife, ain't I? Bought and paid for."

'So they shared the bed, but all they did was sleep.

'Next morning, when the shepherd gets up, he wakes the woman, who starts to get out of bed. "No need to get up," says the shepherd.

' "I've got to get your breakfast," her says. "Light a fire."

' "I've done that for meself for years," he says. "No need for you to get up yet."

'But her did, and while he got the fire going, her fetched water, and got the breakfast together. When he'd eaten, and packed his own midday bit, and got off to his work, the woman had a good look round the house, to see what there was to be done, and what her had to work with. Her found

24

the shepherd's meal chest, and the smoked mutton he had hanging in his chimney. Her found his vegetable patch, and the shed where he stored his vegetables and apples, and her got together everything her had to make a meal with. Her tried hard to remember everything her'd learned from her mother about cooking a good meal. While her'd been wed to the cobbler, her'd forgotten most of what her'd learned, because no matter what her did, whether the meal was good or bad, the cobbler give her a beating – so what was the point in trying hard?

'Anyway, her got a good stew on, to cook slow all through the day, and then her got on and cleaned the house, washed the windows, swept the hearth. Made the bed afresh, took the curtains down, looked through the shepherd's clothes and put aside everything that needed darning, or a button sewed on, or a seam stitching up. Because her'd got a new chance here, and her felt all excited and full of energy.

' "If this one so much as shakes a finger at me," her told her broom, "I'm off!"

'When shepherd come home, he looks round and says, "You've been busy!" And then he sniffs. "And that smells good!"

' "I'll be busier tomorrow," her says. "I shall get on and do some washing." Her was dishing up the stew. "Come and get yourself outside of this. You must be hungry, running round them hills all day."

'The shepherd sits down and starts eating, and he didn't have to say he liked it – anybody could see that. But he says,

"No word of a lie, this is best I've ever tasted."

' "Maybe I'll leave the washing tomorrow and bake instead," says the woman.

' "You can bake?" says shepherd.

' "Of course I can bake. And brew. And sew and spin and knit."

'The shepherd pushes hisself back from the table. "Do you know anything about sheep?"

' "Not a thing," her says. "But I can learn."

' "And your husband knocked you about and sold you for two and six!" says the shepherd.

'Well, after that, they gets on better and better. The shepherd's up first and lights the fire and gets his own breakfast – 'cause after all, he says, he's been used to doing that for years and years, so why shouldn't he go on doing it? And the woman enjoys lying in bed for a while after he's gone, and thinks of how the cobbler would have given her a kicking if her hadn't been up afore him, with his breakfast ready. So, when her does get up, her's thinking fondly of the shepherd, and determined to show him how well her can do things.

'Her bakes a batch of bread to last 'em for a week, and he says you couldn't buy better in a baker's shop. So her has a big laundering day, and takes out the rug and beats it, and he says he's never known the house smell fresher. "It's good to come home these nights," he says. "I can't wait to get in and see what you've cooked for me."

'The woman feels like her's been let out of a dark

cupboard into fresh air and light. Her starts making all sorts of plans. "Next market day," her says, "if we can afford to buy a bit of sugar and a few raisins, I'll bake you a cake. And, if, maybe, we can buy up a few old rags, I could sew some cushions, and make the chairs and settle a bit more comfortable. What d'you think?"

' "I think I got me a clever, clever wife for two and a tanner," he says. And her smiles, pleased at that, and then he says, "A pretty one an' all."

'So then her gets up and goes and sits in his lap; and they start kissing; and after that they don't only sleep in the bed.

'Her got her sugar and raisins and baked her cakes, and shepherd loved 'em. Nobody had baked him a cake since he'd left his mother. Her got her bits of old cloth, and her made some cushions – and the shepherd's socks was all darned so smooth he couldn't feel the mends, and both his shirts had all their buttons and was washed regular. "You look after me," he says.

'And in all this time he never so much as wagged a finger at her. "I'm a lucky man to have so clever a wife," he says; and, "I'm a lucky man to have so pretty a wife." And the woman felt like her was living on strawberries.

'One night her sits down close by him on the settle and says, "I've got something for you." And her puts a bag into his hand, a cloth bag, not very big, but strong material.

' "What's this?" he says.

' "Look and see," her says.

'So he opens the top and looks in – and it's full of coin.

There's silver coin and gold coin – more money than he's ever had in his hand at one time afore. "Where's this come from?" he says.

' "Ah," her says. "That's what I scrimped and saved and stashed away while I was wed to cobbler. It took some doing, and some going hungry and ragged. It cost me some kicks and punches an' all. But there's ninety-eight pounds there. When I had a hundred, I was going to run away."

' "However did you hide it from him?" shepherd says.

' "It was hard," her says. "I had to wear it round me waist all the time, under me clothes – and then, when we undressing for bed, I had to hide it quick, while he wasn't looking. It's been a lot easier hiding it from you."

' "Then why am you showing it to me now?" he says.

' "Why do you think?" her says. "Because I don't want to run away from you. I waited till now, to see what you was going to turn out like. If you'd ever raised your voice to me, or your hand, I should have been off. But you've been so good to me, dear man, I don't think you can be made of the same stuff as me old husband. So I want you to take this money and spend it for the two of we. I was thinking," her says, "that you might buy some sheep of our own with it, instead of just looking after other men's sheep."

' "You saved it," he says, handing it back. "I think you should spend it on yourself. Get yourself some dresses and shoes."

' "Dresses and shoes won't make our fortune," her says. "No. Sheep." And her shoves the money back at him.

' "Tell you what," he says. "Let's split it. I'll buy sheep with half, and you spend the rest on yourself. How's that?"

'So they agreed on that – but though the woman did spend some on cloth to make up into dresses herself, her bought herself a sheep with the rest. And they went on from there, living together, and working together and looking after each other. A flock of sheep and a flock of children.

'The cobbler drunk hisself to death.

'And that might not be much of a story, but it's true, it really happened, not so long ago. When my mother was a girl, her knowed the woman. 'Course, her was an old lady then. But it was her told me mother the story, from her own lips. So that's how I know it's true.'

The women laughed, and rustled the sheets, the blouses, the skirts they were sewing. 'So, Marie, you know what to do if Bobby raises his hand.'

'Or his voice!'

'What?' said Marie. 'Am I to get meself down to the market-place with a halter round me neck?'

Granny Shearing spoke above the laughter and shouting. 'Now it's my turn to tell a story. Shut up, the lot of you, and listen.'

'There was once a young chap as got married. First off, it was all kisses and cuddles and roses in the garden. Then the young chap gets to noticing a weight pressing down on his head all the time. Everywhere he goes, everything he does, there's this weight pressing down on his head. And what is it? It's his wife's thumb.

'So he goes to see his father-in-law. He says, "I want you to take your daughter back."

'His father-in-law says, "What's brought this on?"

'Young chap says, "I'm under her thumb. Her gets her way all the time, and I never get my way. If her wants to visit one friend, that's where we go, even if I want to see somebody else. I have to wear what her wants me to wear, or I never hear the end of it. Her chooses what our money's spent on. I never get a say. And I'm tired of it. I'm tired of being married. I want you to take your daughter back."

' "My dear boy," says the father-in-law, "Till Death do you part and so on. All men are under the thumbs of their wives, didn't you know that? I'm under my wife's thumb. Your father is under your mother's thumb. It's the natural way of things."

' "I don't believe that," says the young chap. "I don't intend to be under my wife's thumb, I can tell you. I want you to take her back."

' "If I can prove to you," says his father-in-law, "that it's the natural way of things for a man to be ruled by his wife, will you be content?"

' "You can't prove any such thing," says the young chap.

' "Listen to me," says the old fella. "I'll provide you with a basket holding a hundred eggs. And from my stable I'll give you five hosses. Five hosses, a hundred eggs. I want you to go out among our neighbours and visit them all, and wherever you find a house where the woman's in charge, there I want you to leave one of your hundred eggs. But whenever you find a house where the husband is master, I want you to give that man his choice from my hosses. Do you follow me?"

' "Yes," says the young chap, "but—"

' "And if you run out of hosses afore you run out of eggs," says the old fella, "I'll take me daughter back."

' "That's easy," says the young chap. "Let's get started!"

'So the young chap and his father-in-law stroll out to the stable-yard, and the old fella rigs the young chap out with a little dog-cart to haul along the basket of one hundred eggs – they get a big basket from the kitchen and a hundred eggs out of store and out of the hen-houses. There's a big dog to pull the little-cart, and there's five hosses out of the stables, and the old fella calls a couple of his stable-hands to help manage 'em. It's quite a parade starts out along the road to see the neighbours.

'First house he comes to, young chap knocks at door, and from inside he hears a woman yell, "Go and answer the door you idle beggar, I can't do everything at once!" Young chap don't bother waiting for the door to be opened. He just leaves an egg on the doorstep and goes on.

'The next house, a man answers the door. The young chap explains why he's going round the neighbourhood with all these hosses, and the dog-cart and the big basket of eggs. The man holds out his hand. "Just give me an egg," he says.

'Next house, the man and woman both come to the door, and the young chap explains what he's doing all over again. "I wear the trousers round here," says the man.

'The woman folds her arms and looks him up and down.

"Do you heck as like," her says, and her unfolds her arms and bats him round the back of the head.

' "If you'll just take this egg," says the young chap, handing her one, "I'll be on my way."

'House after house, it's the same. It's always plain to see that the woman rules the roost, and one by one, the eggs leave the basket. At the end of the day, the young chap, the hosses, the dog and the stable-hands all put up at an inn, and while he's eating his dinner, the young chap listens to the landlady giving orders to everybody in sight and a lot of people out of sight an' all. The landlord never says a word. Keeps his head down. Afore he leaves the next morning, after he's settled the bill, the young chap leaves an egg on the bar.

'The second day's the same as first. Egg after egg gets given away, but there's still five hosses. But then the young chap's luck changes. Him and the stable-hands and the hosses and the dog and the dog-cart all come to a little smallholding, and the young chap knocks at the yard-door. A woman answers it, but as soon as her sees them, her says, "Oh, wait, I'll fetch my husband." And her disappears back into the house.

' "Take as long as you like," says the young chap and stands there at the doorstep, grinning, 'cause he thinks it a good sign that the woman runs off for her husband right away.

'Anyroad, the husband comes to door. "What can I do for you?" he says. His wife stands just behind him, peering round his shoulder, listening.

'Young chap explains why he's come, all about giving away eggs to households where the woman rules, but letting any man who's in charge of his own family take his pick from these five very fine hosses.

'The smallholder starts grinning afore he's finished talking. "Ah, well, I reckon I gain hoss, then," he says. "I always have the last word round here, don't I, Jenny?"

' "Aye, you do," says his wife, looking up at him.

' "First word and last," says the smallholder, and his wife nods.

'Young chap's delighted. "Please," he says. "Choose your hoss." He thinks he'll be rid of all the hosses in no time now.

'Smallholder steps into yard and starts looking over all the hosses. His wife follows him out, and stands watching, her hands folded in front of her. Her don't say nothing, just watches.

' "Well," says smallholder, when he's had a good look, "I think I'll take the black gelding, he's a good strong hoss, just what I need."

' "The grey mare's very nice, John," says his wife.

' "Very nice," he says. "Very pretty little mare, but not what I'm in need of. The black gelding is."

' "The grey mare'd make a lovely mount for me to go to church and round the neighbourhood," says his wife.

' "I daresay it would," says her husband, "but the black gelding is the one we're taking."

' "You know best," says the wife. But tears start running down her face.

' "Oh, *all right*!" says her husband. "Don't cry! We'll take the grey mare instead!"

' "Oh no, you won't," says young chap. "You'll take an egg." And away he goes, with the five hosses, and the stable-hands, and the dog pulling the cart holding what's left of the eggs.

'Which he soon got rid of.

'The five hosses he had to take back to his father-in-law.

'And he had to keep his wife.

'And he was under her thumb until the day he died.

'That's my story. Tell me there ain't a word of truth in it!'

The women laughed, and stitched and snipped, and brewed another pot of tea.

Two

Leaving Home

Polly stood with her back against the door. Letty marked her height on the lintel and said, 'When you come home, we'll see how much you've grown. We're all going to miss you. Your mother'll miss you, I know as much.'

'I shall have one Sunday off every month,' Polly said. 'I'll come home then and see everybody.' She was twelve years old, and was to start work the next day as a maid at an inn. Every morning she would rise early to clear grates of ashes and light new fires. She would scrub floors, and sweep and polish them, fetch water, wash dishes, peel potatoes, change beds, and do anything else required of her, from dawn until after dark, every day.

'Ah, but soon you'll find yourself a young man,' said Granny Shearing. She cut a length of wool and threaded it into her darning needle. A pile of darning was heaped on the floor at her feet, and while she talked, she worked. 'You won't bother tramping all this way to see us then.'

'I shall miss everybody,' Polly said, and screwed up her face and sobbed.

Letty hugged her. 'Never mind, never mind. It comes to we all – we all must leave home, and work, and make our own way . . .'

'Let's have a story!' said Clo. In her lap was a heap of daisies, white, pink, green and yellow, and she wove them into a chain. 'Take our minds off her going. I know one. I know a good un. Listen . . .'

'There was this wench – call her Joan – and her hadn't got no father and, soon as her was growed, her mother throwed her out. "Stand on your own two feet and don't come running snivelling to me no more. Earn your own bread, and see how you like it."

'So Joan wanders off into the big world. Whichever way her goes, it's all the same to her – there's nobody waiting for her at the end of any of 'em: no roof to shelter her, no fire to warm her, no dinner waiting for her, no bed.

'Her comes to a deep, wild wood, full of bears and wolves, and her wanders through it by little twisty paths, through all green darkness, with thorns scratching at her, not knowing if her's going to live to see another day. And when her sees a little cottage with a candle burning in its window, her's so thankful. Her goes up to the door and knocks, and when a woman answers it, Joan says, "Please may I come in and sleep here the night? I'll do any work you've got to do, if I can sleep here instead of in the wood."

' "You'd be safer in the wood, me love," says the woman. "A bunch of robbers live here. Desperate types. They'd slit your gizzard soon as look at you. If I was you, I'd take to me heels while I had the chance."

' "There's bears out here, and wolves," says Joan, "and I've had nothing to eat and I don't like the dark. Let me come in, please. I'll take me chances with the robbers."

' "It's your funeral," says the woman, and lets Joan in to sit by the fire, and gives her some bread and cheese to eat. Joan golluped it down.

'It was hell-squealing time when the robbers come home. They all come ducking in through the door, all of 'em as big and hairy as bears. One's had his nose cut off, and one's had his ear cut off, and all of 'em have got teeth knocked out, and scars all over their faces. Fearful rough lot, they are. And when they see Joan sitting by the fire, they say,

' "Who's this?"

' "What's this? you mean."

' "It's too skinny to be any use."

' "Throw it in the cook-pot – its bones might boil down to a stock."

'Then Joan stands up, puts her hands on her hips and says, "You'd better mind your manners round me. I'm the Queen of Thieves."

' "Ooh!" they say.

' "Ooh, Your Majesty! Forgive us!"

' "Here, Your Majesty, put on your crown!" And one of the robbers puts an upturned chamberpot on her head, and they all laughed at her.

' "Her's hungry and tired," says the robbers' housekeeper. "Let her stay here the night."

' "Only if her sleeps by the fire," say the robbers, "and takes herself off tomorrow. We've no use for scrawny little kids."

'So Joan has to sleep on the hard floor by the fire, and the room gets colder and colder as the fire goes out. Her has to spread out the warm ashes and lie in 'em to keep warm, and the next morning, when the housekeeper wakes her, her's filthy.

' "Well, m'wench," says the housekeeper, "you've got to go." And her gives her a crust of bread, and shows her the door while the robbers am still lifting their blankets with their snores.

'So Joan's out on the road again, with no friends and nowhere to go. Her trudges along and comes on a road where a farmer was herding a flock of sheep. Her calls out to the farmer, "I need work. You got any?"

'All the farmer sees is this scrawny little wench, all filthy from the ashes her's slept in, so he gives her a hard look, and goes on without so much as a nod.

'Right, says Joan to herself. I'm going to have to look after myself, I can see.

'So her leaves the road and goes into the wood, and her runs through the trees alongside the road until her gets ahead of the farmer and the sheep. Then her takes off her shoes, cleans one of them up with some leaves, and throws it onto the road where the farmer'll see it.

'Up comes the farmer, driving his sheep, and sees the shoe lying in the road. Looks like a nice shoe, he thinks, but there's only the one. On he goes.

'Joan runs through the trees again, until her's ahead of him. Then her throws her other shoe into the road. And her hides in the wood.

'Along comes the farmer with his sheep, and sees the shoe lying there. "That's the other shoe," he thinks. "Somebody's lost both of 'em." And he stops and picks up the shoe. The sheep go wandering on along the road.

'The farmer turns the shoe over and has a good look at it. "That'd do for our Alice," he thinks. Well, shoes am expensive. He thinks, "I'll just nip back along the road and see whether that other shoe and this one make a pair." And back along the road he goes, leaving his sheep.

'Joan comes out of the wood and drives the sheep away into the trees, and down the road to the robbers' cottage. Her knocks on the door and shouts, "Come out! Come out and see what the Queen of Thieves has thieved!"

'Out come all the robbers and their housekeeper, and they see this flock of sheep that Joan's pinched all by herself. And they start nodding and pulling their beards and saying, "That is clever. No, credit where credit's due. You've got to admit, that's talent." And they invite Joan into their cottage, and give her a place by the fire, and share their food with her. And, that night, they make up a bit of a bed for her by the fire.

' "This is a sight better than being on the road," Joan thinks to herself.

'Next day, early, her takes a big crust of bread for her breakfast, and goes off into the wood to see what her can see.

Her comes on the same farmer, only this time he's driving an ox. Joan follows him, hiding amongst the trees, and thinking hard how her can get the ox.

'Her finds a rope lying in the leaves, and gets an idea. Her runs ahead of the farmer, climbs into a tree, and takes off her shawl. The rope her makes into a kind of harness, tying it round her waist and shoulders – the other end her ties, very tight, to a branch. Then her hides the rope harness by wrapping her shawl round herself, and just hangs there, dangling from this tree, for all the world as if her'd been hung for sheep-stealing.

'Along comes the farmer, with his ox. He looks up and sees this girl, hung. "Another thieving scallywag got what her deserves," he thinks, and goes on. When he's out of sight, Joan unties herself, climbs down from the tree and runs on until her's ahead of him again. Then her climbs into another tree, and hangs herself up there, just like before.

'Along comes the farmer. "That girl hanging there looks just like the one we passed a while back," he says to the ox, and he stops and looks up at Joan for a bit. Then he shakes his head. "No, couldn't be," he says, and goes on.

'Joan unties herself, climbs down, runs ahead of him, climbs into another tree, and hangs herself again. Along comes farmer. "Swipe me," he says to his ox. "There's another one, looks just like the first two. Did they hang triplets?" He stands there wondering about it for a bit, then he says, "I shall have to go back and have a look at them other two, to make sure. If I don't, I shall never stop thinking about it." So he leaves the ox tethered to a tree, and he goes back up the road to have another look at these hanged wenches.

'Down from her tree comes Joan, unties the ox, and leads it off to the robbers' cottage. "Come out, come out and see what I've got this time," her says.

'Out all the robbers come, and they're very taken with this fine ox.

' "We can sell that at market for a fair few quid," says one.

' "I think you must be the Queen of Thieves, lass," says another, and the others all nod and nod.

' "Join we," they say. "Be one of we." And Joan's very glad to do it.

'Next day, her's up early again and off into the wood. And along comes the same farmer. This time he's riding hoss. So Joan goes through the wood alongside the road, and her makes noises like sheep and like an ox. Farmer thinks it's his sheep and his ox he can hear, lost in the wood. So he gets off his hoss, ties it to a tree, and goes into the wood to see if he can find 'em. Joan comes out of the wood, unties the hoss, and rides it back to the robbers' cottage.

' "You am the Queen of Thieves, and no doubt!" say the robbers, and they give her a seat at table with 'em, and a proper bed of her own.

' "Now you're one of we," they say, "we ought to show you where we keep all our treasure." So they light lanterns, and lead her deep into the wood to a cave with a big iron door and seven locks. They show her where they hide the keys, and they open the big iron door, and inside there's boxes of gold coin, and jewels, and crowns, and gold and silver plates, all piled up.

' "I'll never tell a living soul where this cave is," says Joan. "I promise." And her keeps her promise.

'After that Joan lived with the robbers for a bit, and they all got on together – but pretty soon the robbers say they want to go to a fair that's come to a town a day's travel away. There'll be plenty of people coming to the fair with pockets full of money, and going home with pockets full of money from selling their wares, and the robbers can rob the people coming and going . . . and they can have a bit of fun an' all, winning coconuts and eating gobstoppers. Even robbers want to have a bit of fun once in a while.

' "Come with we, Joanie," they say. "We'll treat you to a ride on a donkey and buy you a banana."

' "Can I have me photo took an' all?" Joan asks, and pretends to be all excited about going – but when the day of the fair comes round, her complains that her's sick. Her head aches, her says; her guts am griping. "Poor wench," say the robbers. "Shall we stop home with you?"

' "No, no," says Joan. "I shall be all right. I don't want to spoil your day. I wish I could come an' all, but I just don't feel well enough."

'They all believe her, 'cos her seemed so keen to go before. Off all the robbers go, with their housekeeper, to the fair. Soon as they've gone, up gets Joan. Her wasn't ill at all. Away her goes to the robbers' cave, finds the keys, opens it up, and fills her pockets and her shawl and her boots with coin and jewels.

Her fetches the hoss her stole from the farmer, and loads him up with more treasure, and leads him off. On her way, her calls in at the farmer's house, and tells him where he'll find his sheep and his ox, and gives him a good price for his hoss.

'Joan took herself a good, long way off, to a town where nobody knowed her, and bought herself a smart little house and settled down to be happy. And so her was, for a long while. Her did a bit of this, a bit of that, turned a little penny here, and another there and went on very well until her decided that what her hadn't got, and what her wanted, was a husband.

'Don't her know when her's well off?' asked Granny Shearing. 'Last thing in this world her wants is husband.'

'You've had three,' said Clo.

'Took me a long while to learn sense,' said the old woman.

'Go on with the story,' said Polly.

'Well it happened,' said Clo, 'that, in that part of the country, there was a squire. He was rich, he was good-looking, he was young, and he was single. 'He's the one for me,' says Joan. So her invites him round for dinner.

'Squire's willing enough, 'cos Joan's a pretty girl. And then, her little house is comfortable, and the meal her serves him is all of the best. Joan tells him how her outdid the robbers, and makes him laugh, and he's flirting with her and enjoying hisself – until her says, "Will you marry me?"

'That gives him a shock. He says, "I suppose I've got to marry, one day – but I wasn't planning on it being any day soon."

43

' "No rush," her says. "So long as we'm married by next year."

'He laughs and says, "Well, you're a witty woman – but can you outwit me?"

' "Try me," her says.

' "I'll set you three tasks," he says. "Complete 'em, and I'll marry you. My word on it."

' "Book the church for the wedding," says Joan, "and tell me first task."

' "On Sunday, I shall be giving a dinner meself," says Squire. "I'd invite you, but you'll be busy. If you can come to my house and steal a goose from the spit in my kitchen, while all my staff are on guard against you – well, that's the first task."

' "I feel sorry for your guests," her says. "They're going to be getting bread and cheese when they expected fat goose."

' "We shall see," says Squire, and home he goes to tell all his staff about the bet he's made with Madam Joan – only he says it's a bet for money, not for marriage. They've got to be watchful on Sunday, and never take their eyes off the geese on the spit, so that Joan can't sneak in and steal one. "If Sunday comes and goes without me losing a goose," he says, "I'll give you each a gold guinea."

'Well, the days pass and Sunday comes round. The kitchen staff are all excited and on guard. Madam Joan ain't going to get by them. There's one young skivvy who's taken away from all other work and just stood by the hearth to watch the geese turning on the spit, to make sure.

'But while they'm all being so careful in the kitchen, into

the yard of the squire's house comes a skinny young fella, his chin all dirty with stubble, carrying a twitching sack. He gets talking to the stable-lads. In this sack, he says, he's got three hares. Good eating. If he took 'em up to the kitchens, do they think the cook would buy 'em?

'Oh, I dunno, says the stable-lad. Cook usually buys only the best, from the butcher in town.

' "But these am really good, fat hares," says the beggar-lad, and he opens the top of the sack, to show the stable-lads – and out jumps one of the hares!

'It hares round the yard, looking for a way out, and the dog chained outside the kitchen door barks like a mad thing, yanking at its chain, making a terrible noise. And the dogs that hang round the stables all chase the hare, all barking, snapping and yapping – and the cats hiss and growl – and all the hens cluck and the ducks quack and beat their wings.

'In the kitchen, everybody wonders what the uproar's about, and a few of the servants forget all about watching the geese on the spit, and run out into the yard. But the cook shouts out, "Watch the geese!" And the rest stop put.

'Out in the yard, the beggar-lad opens his sack again, and lets out a second hare. The hubbub's worse than before. More dogs come into the yard from the street and start fighting with Squire's dogs. The horses in the stables are neighing and kicking. The stable-lads are yelling. The servants from the kitchen are screeching.

'Out comes the squire, shouting, "What's all this about?" And people are yelling back, trying to explain. And more people are coming into the yard, because they can hear the row.

'More of the kitchen staff come running out into the yard, because the uproar's so bad they feel sure the house is burning down, or somebody's being murdered, and they've just got to see. But cook shouts to the skivvy, "Just watch them geese!" And the skivvy and cook stay put.

'Now the beggar-lad edges through the crowd, right over to the door of the kitchen. And he lets the last of the hares go through the kitchen door. Round the tables the hare goes streaking, and the cook yells, "Aargh! What's that? A rat?" And into the kitchen come dogs, and they chase the hare all over, all between the table legs, fighting each other, and barking and snarling, and the skivvy runs away in a fright, and other people run in with sticks and tools, to drive the dogs out.

'And when, at last, the dogs and the hare have been chased out of the kitchen, and people have stopped yelling and screaming, and tables have been stood on their legs again, and the skivvy's been found and set to mopping up the mess of things spilt and smashed on the kitchen floor – when everything's calmed down a bit, what do they find? Why, that the geese have gone from the spit. Not just one of the geese, but all of 'em. And not only the geese have gone, neither. Loaves of bread, and a game pie, and a tray of cakes and dainties have gone as well.

'Soon as Squire's told of this, he goes straight to Joan's house, and there her is, all pretty and neat in a frock; and on her sideboard are the geese, on a platter, and the game pie, and the cakes and dainties. They're a bit knocked about, but there they are.

' "How did you do it?" says Squire.

' "That's for me to know and you to figure out," her says. "What's your next task?"

' "It'll be harder," says Squire, and he sits down and thinks for a while. Then he says, "Tomorrow night there'll be six hosses in my stable. Every one'll have a man sitting on his back. If you can steal the hosses without hurting the men, that'll be the second task."

' "Tomorrow night?" says Joan.

' "Tomorrow night."

' "That don't give me much time to plan," her says.

' "All the harder, then," says Squire. "Remember, you're not to hurt the men."

' "I've never hurt anybody," her says. "Hurt 'em? I won't even wake 'em."

'Next night, in Squire's stable, all warm and smelling of hay, there are the six hosses with the six men on their backs. At first they're all wide awake, and ready to think that even a mouse is Madam Joan in disguise.

' "That beggar-lad with the hares in a sack," says one. "D'you reckon that was her?"

' "Might have been," says another. "Or her might just have paid him to create a fuss."

' "Or her took her chance and snuck in while everybody was running round like mad things," says another one.

' "Well, any skinny beggar-lads come in here with

sacks," says the first, "we'm ready for 'em!"

'But nobody come. Hours went by, went slowly, slowly by, and nothing at all happened. First the men got bored, and then they got tired, and then they was bored and tired.

' "Here," says one, taking a flask out of his pocket. "Have a nip of this."

' "I thought we had orders not to drink," says another. "We've got to be sharp."

'The first one's taking a good drink from the flask. "Ar, but nothing's going to happen now," he says. "It's almost morning." And he passes the flask round and they all have a swig.

'Then they hear the stable door scrape along the ground as it's opened, and they all sit up straight on their hosses' backs and look round. In through the stable-door comes a fat old woman, all bundled up in skirts and shawls, with grey hair bursting out from under an old cap. "Ooh!" her says in surprise, when her sees six men sitting on six hosses in the stalls. "Oh, I'm sorry," her says. "I didn't know anybody was in here. I was just looking for somewhere out of the wind to have a little sleep."

'Well, the six men look at her hard, and they look at each other. But the old woman sounded so shocked to see 'em, and her was such a dirty, scruffy, *fat* old woman, that they didn't think her could be Madam Joan.

' "Oh, come in, Mother," says one of the men. "Nobody'll bother you here."

' "Thank you," her says. "You'm good boys." And

her crawls into a pile of straw to sleep.

' "We should search her," whispers one of the men. "Make sure her ain't Madam Joan."

' "Don't be daft," say the others. "How can we search an old woman like that? Wouldn't be respectful. 'Sides, her don't look nothing like Madam Joan."

'After a while the old woman sits up and hunts through her clothes until her finds an old flask, and her takes a drink from it. "I'm too cold, I can't sleep," her says. "A drink'll warm me up." Then her holds out the flask to the six men. "D'you want a sup?"

' "Thank you kindly," says one of the men, to be friendly. "You have some of ours." So the old woman gets up and comes over to the hosses, and her swops flasks with the men. Her drinks from their flask, and they pass her flask from one to the other of 'em, and they all drink.

'And the next thing, they all fall asleep, their heads sinking down on their hosses's necks. 'Cos the old woman is Joan, and the flask her gives them is full of a strong sleeping draught – her only pretended to drink from it herself. And the men are already a bit drunk, and they fall asleep between one breath and the next.

'Well then, Joan gets busy. Her takes the first man down from his hoss – he's heavy, but her manages it – and her lays him down, still asleep, in the straw. Then her leads his hoss out of its stall and tethers it near the stable door. Then her takes the second man down, and puts him to sleep in the straw, and leads his hoss to the door – and so on, until all six

49

men are sleeping in the straw, and her back's near breaking with the work, and all six hosses are waiting by the door. Then her leads all six away to her own house. Her has quite a job handling all six of 'em, but her gets 'em there. Her stables ain't big enough for all six, but her gets three of 'em in, and her tethers the others in the yard with blankets over 'em, and puts hay for 'em to eat.

'Next morning Squire goes down to his stables and finds his six hosses gone, and his six men snoring in the straw. "Looks like I'd better resign meself to getting married," he says to hisself. Round he goes to Joan's house, and her takes him through to her yard and stables, and there are all his hosses, stolen from under the arses of his men.

' "Two down and one to go," says Joan. "What's your last task? And have you booked the church yet?"

'The Squire says, "D'you know the vicar of St Tom's?"

' "I do," says Joan, "and what I know of him, I don't like."

' "I agree with you," says Squire. "Always insists on his tithe, whether folk can pay it or not – insists on it to the last penny, the last egg, the last ear of wheat. And what does he do in return? Gives sermons ten minutes long, so he's got time to go hunting. Won't go out to visit the dying at night or if he doesn't feel like it. I'd like to see that man taken down a peg or two."

' "Is that my last task?" says Joan.

' "I want to see the vicar of St Tom's give all his goods away to the poor, and turn over a new leaf," says Squire. "Can you do that?"

' "We shall see," says Joan; and they part.

'Joan starts watching the vicar, and stirring up all sorts of gossip about him, so her can learn his ways. Her finds out what time he gets up in the morning, and how he spends his day, and what roads he goes by, and which he comes back by, and an awful lot more about him. Her learns, for one thing, that he spends every evening sitting in his house by the church, getting drunk as a lordly newt. He won't go to the pub like everybody else, 'cos he don't want folk to see him getting drunk. No, he buys his booze in the next town – robbing the locals of his money – and he brings it back with him and drinks it in his front parlour.

'So Joan has a think, and her goes to town herself, and buys a few things – like a lot of sequins, and some wire, and a bicycle lamp – and then her goes home and does some work. Her rigs the bicycle lamp up so her can switch it on by pulling a string; and her makes herself a long white dress, all stitched with sequins. With the wire her makes a pair of wings, and her covers them with sequins and tinsel an' all, and her makes a halo to stand up behind her head on a wire, and her covers the halo with gold tinsel, and hangs lots of little sequins off it, so they tremble and catch the light.

'Then, after dark, her sneaks out to the churchyard, and her hangs the bicycle lamp up in a tree, and pulls on the string to make sure it works – and sure enough, on it comes and shines a strong bright light over the gravestones. Then her switches it off again and, in the dark, puts on her white robe, and her wings and her halo. When her's all dressed up, her goes over to the vicar's house and creeps up to the window. Her can see him inside, sitting in his chair, a bottle by his side and a glass in his hand. His collar's undone, and he looks all red-faced and tipsy.

'Joan crouches down by the window and starts to call his name. "Sacherveral St John Davids," her shouts – that was his name – "come out and face your reckoning!" Her shouts this two or three times, and then hears the vicar getting up, all noisy and clumsy, so her nips into the shrubbery by the window. The vicar opens the window and looks out. "Who's there?" he shouts. "You'll laugh on the other side of your face if I have to come out to you!"

'He gets no answer, and soon stumbles back to his chair and his drinking. But, o'course, soon as he's settled, Joan's back at the window, calling him again. Her makes her voice all hollow and moany, like a spirit. "Come out – come out and face your reckoning! Come out, Sacherveral!"

'Now the vicar's angry, and he gets up, all in a rush, and Joan hears him stamping out into the hallway. So her lifts up her robes and runs back to where her's hung the bicycle lamp in the tree, and her gets hold of the string that turns it on.

'Out comes the vicar, tottering about and almost falling over. "I'm going to ding your ears when I catch you!" he shouts. "I'll give it you, disturbing me!"

'Then Joan pulls the string and switches on the bicycle lamp, and it shines a strong white light right into the vicar's eyes. He stops dead, surprised and a bit scared, and he tries to cover his eyes. But all he can see is a white dazzle, and in this dazzle there's a figure dressed all in a long, shining, glittering white robe, with two shining, sparkling wings, and a golden, shimmering halo round its head.

' "Sacherveral," says this figure sadly, and it shakes its head so that its halo shimmers. "I'm a messenger from heaven, come to tell you that your time on earth is almost over."

' "Oh no!" cries the vicar, and his legs give way and he sits down on the churchyard path. He's so drunk, he believes it all.

' "Oh yes," says the angel, "and you know and I know that you haven't lived as you should. I've come to warn you that, unless you mend your ways, the devil will soon be pitchforking you by your tender bits into one of his cauldrons."

' "What can I do?" says vicar. "Angel, tell me what I can do to make up for my wicked life."

' "Do as Christ told you to do," says angel. "Give away your goods to the poor. All those tithes that you made people pay, that have crammed your barn full – what good is it to you now? Think on the fires of Hell, Sacherveral, think on."

'Then the angel, shimmering and shining, drifts over to a tree, and suddenly the Heavenly Light that shone around it goes out, and the angel's not there any more. Vicar's too scared and troubled to hear feet running off in the dark. He goes back into his house, all of a tremble, thinking he's really seen a Heavenly Vision.

'Next day, when he wakes up with a headache and a dry mouth, he sits up in bed and thinks about what he saw. It must have been a vision, he thinks. He reckons he's too clever to be fooled by anybody, see, and he reckons he don't drink much — so what he saw must have been real. Which means he has to give all his goods away to the poor.

'So he gives away all his clothes and shoes until he's only got what he stands up in, and one change. And then he sells all his knick-knacks, and fine glassware and china, and books and carpets and so on, and he gives away the money he gets for it all. And he sends out word that anybody who's in need of food can come to him, and he'll give 'em grain out of his tithe-barn.

'Squire says to Joan, "The church's been booked for weeks, in the next town. The bans have been called. We can be married tomorrow, if you still want to."

' "Suits me," says Joan, and married they was, and lived long and happily together, with the squire always taking his wife's advice. He reckoned, if her couldn't find a way round something, there was no way round it.

'Snip, snap, snout, that's *that* tale told out.'

'So cheer up, cheer up,' Letty said, and cuddled Polly again. 'You'll make your little fortune and find your squire—'

'Well, I never found neither,' said Granny Shearing.

'Oh, you shut up,' said Letty. 'Don't you listen to her, my love. Her's had a good long life—'

'Hardship and heartache,' said Granny Shearing. 'If I told you my story, it'd have you all crying.'

'Her's had her moments,' said Letty. 'Her's kicked her heels up.'

'I wouldn't change any of it,' Granny Shearing admitted.

'Auntie Letty,' said Polly. 'Will you tell a story?'

Letty thought for a while. 'Well, the only one I can think of just now is this one . . .

'This happened years ago, when times was hard. There was no work, and no money, and folk was living on Waterloo porridge – that's what the soldiers et on the battlefield at Waterloo when they couldn't build no fires to cook. It's just flour or oatmeal stirred into cold water. Folk was so hard up they hadn't got money to buy coal or wood for fires to cook food, see, and they couldn't afford nothing but flour. Miserable times. Don't let nobody tell you about the good old days when everything was wonderful and everybody was happy. There wasn't never no such time.

'Anyroad, there was these two blokes – they was named Jack and Joe – and they left their wives and children behind and set out on the tramp, to find work. They trudged on for days, and got nothing. At night they slept in doorways or hedges, and started tramping again early the next morning.

'This one night – it was getting dark – they found theirselves right out in the country with no towns or villages near, no houses or even a barn where they could shelter. Then, against the sky, they see this tower standing: an old-ruined castle.

' "Let's head for there," says Jack. "There might be a roof left, or some corner we can get out the wind. Better than nothing."

'Joe agreed, so they climbed up to the tower. When they got to it, the roof was still on, and there was a good-sized, dry

55

room at the bottom. "We'm in luck," Joe says, and they settled down to spend the night. They was so tired, after walking all day, that they soon fell asleep, even though they was lying on the hard floor.

'Seemed like they'd hardly closed their eyes, though, afore they was waked up again. Something outside was yowling and screeching and wailing and coming closer, and there was bright firelight, from burning torches, coming in through the tower's doorway. Joe and Jack huddled together in a corner, thinking they was going to be eaten alive.

'In through tower door comes a company of cats. Black cats, white cats, black-and-white cats, tabby cats, ginger cats, grey cats. They'm all singing, and carrying burning torches, and leading 'em is the biggest cat of all, a big black cat, wearing a gold crown between his ears: the King of the Cats.

'A white cat spreads a tablecloth on the floor, and as soon as it's spread, the tablecloth's covered with food. There's roasted chickens and roasted pheasants, mounds of eggs, bowls of milk and cream, whole baked carp and trout and salmon.

'The King of the Cats sees the two men, and he says, "Come and join we – be our guests. Eat and drink your fill."

'Well, Joe and Jack didn't need asking twice. They come over to where the tablecloth's spread, and they got stuck in, piling their golden plates with fish and meat, pushing whole eggs into their mouths, and pouring theirselves big crystal glasses full of milk.

' "Is there anything you'd like that you don't see here?"
says the King of Cats.

' "If you please, Your Majesty," says Joe, "I fancy some
green peas. And potatoes."

' "I'd like some cake," says Jack. "Some currant cake."

' "And if you're not teetotal," says Joe, "I'd like some beer."

'The King of Cats puts his paw on the tablecloth, and says,
"Let their wishes be answered." Right away there's all sorts
of vegetables – carrots and cabbage and beans and asparagus,
as well as potatoes and peas – and sponge cake, and ginger-
bread and chocolate cake as well as currant cake – and beer in
a jug, and a bottle of whisky. The two blokes tried to thank
the King of Cats as well as they could with their mouths full.

' "It's my pleasure to entertain my guests," says the King.
"Now tell me what you're doing here, in this lonely place, at
a time when men are usually snoring in their beds?"

'So Joe and Jack tell him about how they're looking for
work, and about all their troubles, and how they've got
families going hungry.

' "A sad tale," says the King. "You must have this
tablecloth. Then your families will never be hungry again."

' "Oh, Your Majesty—!" they say. They can't say nothing
else. They're too astonished.

' "Never think of it for a minute," says the King of Cats,
waving a paw. "I've got others. But if it's work you're
needing, I know a job that needs doing. One that'd be well
paid too,"

' "Tell us, Your Majesty!" says Jack.

' "The King of this country," says King of Cats, "the King of men in this country, I mean, has a sick daughter. He's offering to give half his treasure to anybody who can cure her."

' "That'd be all very well if we was doctors, Your Majesty," says Joe, "but we ain't."

' "You don't need to be," says King of Cats, " 'cause I know what's wrong with the Princess. Her's got three kittens inside her. Once her's rid of them, her'll be right as rain."

' "And do you know how to rid her of 'em?" Jack asks.

' "I do," says the King of Cats. "Behind this old tower there's a garden, though you wouldn't know it, it's so over-grown. In amongst all them bushes and weeds and brambles, there's an old well, a magic well. Give the Princess three drinks of water from that well, and her'll soon be over her trouble."

'Joe and Jack look at each other. "Well," says Joe.

' "Your Majesty," says Jack.

' "We don't know how to thank you."

' "For being so good to we."

' "Forget it," says the King of Cats. "Think of it as my way of thanking you for the pleasure of your company tonight."

'Joe, Jack and all the cats feasted until morning come, and then the cats wailed and screeched goodbye, and run off into the wild thorns and bushes round the tower. Joe and Jack was left with the tablecloth spread on the floor, all covered with left-overs. They sit looking at it, and then Jack put his hand on the cloth and said, "Everything clear away!" And all the plates and cups and bowls and food and glasses and bottles vanished, leaving the tablecloth empty. They folded it up, and Jack put it in his pack.

' "I wonder, will we have to wash up the plates next time," says Joe, "or will they come back clean?"

' "We shall see," says Jack, "but first, we've got to find that well."

'So they goes outside and wanders round the tower, and like the King of Cats said, it's hard to tell where any garden might have been – but they've got tools in their packs, in case they find work, and they spend a whole day cutting back the thorns and bushes, until they find the well, and fill their water-bottles from it. They'm hungry after all that work, so they spread the magic tablecloth on the floor of the tower again, and Jack says, "Roast beef and all the trimmings!" And Joe says, "Steak and kidney pudding!" And the tablecloth serves both of 'em what they want. And they don't have to do no washing up neither.

'Next day, they'm up and on the tramp early. They trudge all the way to the King's castle, go up to the gate, and say they've come to cure the Princess. Well, they'm so dirty and scruffy, nobody wants to let 'em in, but they won't go away, and keep hanging round the castle gate, saying that they can cure the Princess, and only they can, nobody else. The King comes to hear of it, and he's so desperate to see his daughter well, that he orders his servants to let Joe and Jack in, and they'm brought before him.

' "You're the two worst-dressed, filthiest, most bedraggled

doctors I've ever seen," he says. "Do you still declare, to my face, that you can cure my daughter?"

' "Are you still offering half your treasure if we can?" says Jack.

' "I am: but if you fail, I think I'll cut off your heads for your impudence," says the King.

'So Joe and Jack were taken in to see the Princess. Her was in bed, looking very poorly, with a swollen belly. "Never mind, m'love," says Jack. "Have a drink of this, and you'll soon be better. Have three big swigs."

'So the Princess had her three drinks of cold well-water, and then her had kittens, and after that her was all better – in fact, better than her'd been afore.

' "Well, you've been as good as your word," says the King, "so I'll be as good as mine." And he opened up his treasure-house and give 'em half his treasure.

'So there they was, rich as rich – but they had a disagree-ment. Jack wanted to go straight back home to their families, but Joe thought they ought to give the well-water they had left to the sick, to see if it would cure 'em. "We'm made for life now," he says. "Got no more worries. So we ought to do what we can for them not as fortunate."

' "You do your ministering to the sick," says Jack, "and I'll go home."

'So that's settled. Jack has most of the treasure loaded into a big coach, and off he sets back home, promising that he'll make sure Joe's family get their share of the treasure.

'Joe keeps a hundred pounds in gold, and the magic

tablecloth, to feed him, and he wanders about from town to town and village to village. All the sick folk come to him, and he gives 'em a drink from his flask of well-water – and it does cure 'em, of all sorts of afflictions: sore eyes and swollen necks, aching joints and griping bellies. He eases a lot of pain, but he's missing his family, and when he runs out of well-water, Joe reckons he's done enough good deeds, and sets off home on foot.

'On the way he meets an old tramp, who begs him for a few pennies to buy hisself a loaf of bread. "I can do better than that," says Joe, and he spreads the tablecloth by the side of the road. "What d'you fancy?" he asks.

' "Bread and cheese'll do," says the tramp.

' "Grant his wish," says Joe, and the tablecloth covers itself with the best french bread, half a dozen different cheeses, grapes, apples and fresh peaches, and white wine. The tramp eats until he aches, and then says, "I'll do a swop with you for this tablecloth."

' "What can you swop me?" Joe says.

'The old tramp pulls a bottle out of his pocket. It just looks like a beer bottle. He puts it down on the ground and he says, "Present arms!" And up out of the neck of the bottle come swarming – like ants – scores of tiny soldiers with tiny gold buttons flashing and little bayonets in their tiny rifles. The further they got from the bottle, the bigger they growed, until they was full sized men, forming up into squads.

' "They'll do whatever you tell 'em," says the old tramp.

' "Then why didn't you tell 'em to get you some food?" says Joe.

' "Oh, I never thought o'that," says tramp. He's not what you'd call the clearest glass of beer. "If you give me the tablecloth, I shan't need 'em anyroad, shall I?" he says.

' "Done!" says Joe. "It's a swop."

' "Back to barracks!" says the tramp, and all the soldiers run back into the bottle, shrinking as they go. Joe folds the tablecloth up, and gives it to the tramp. The bottle he puts in his own pocket, and off they go, by different roads.

'But as Joe's walking along, he starts thinking: I was a fool to give up that tablecloth. He thinks, no matter how rich you are, a tablecloth like that's worth having. If I didn't need it meself, I could feed the poor with it. I'd make better use of it than that old tramp, who'll only eat hisself sick with it.

'And the end of it is, Joe puts the bottle on the ground and says, "Present arms!"

'Out of the bottle come all the soldiers, running in all directions and growing as they run, until they'm all full sized and formed up in ranks. Their Captain salutes Joe and says, "What's your orders, sir?"

' "Go back down the road a piece," says Joe, "find that old tramp, and get the tablecloth back off him. Don't hurt him, mind. And give him this hundred pounds.

'Off go the soldiers, marching, left, right, left, right, and in an hour they'm back, and the Captain salutes and presents Joe with the tablecloth. Joe spreads it on the floor and says, "Let's have a feast!" – just to check that it is the right tablecloth.

'A grand feast appears, and Joe lets all the soldiers eat all they want – well, they can't have much of a life, living in a bottle. They eat so much, he's surprised they can still fit back inside the bottle, but they do, and he puts the bottle and the tablecloth in his pack, and goes on his way.

'He gets back to his own town, and thinks he'll just go back to his old home, to ask the neighbours where his wife's moved to. Her won't be living there any more, he thinks – Jack will have given her a share of the treasure, and her'll have moved somewhere better. But when he gets back to his old house, he finds his wife and children still living there, as poor and hungry as ever.

' "What have you done with the money?" he says.

' "What money?" her says. "Did you send me some? It ain't got here."

' "I've made us rich," he said. "Jack was bringing you our share. What's happened to it?"

' "Jack?" her says. "Oh, Jack won't talk to we now. You won't have heard, but he's the mayor and thinks hisself too good for we these days. He swanks round in a big motor-car with a gold chain round his neck, and his wife's got a fur coat and diamond earrings."

'Well, when Joe heard that, you know how mad he was. He went straight off to the town hall, where the mayor lived, meaning to ask Jack what the hell he meant by robbing his friends. But the guards at the town hall wouldn't let him in, and the mayor – that's Jack – sent word out that he'd never heard of Joe and didn't owe him a penny, and if he didn't go away and stop making trouble, he'd have him throwed in jail.

'So what did Joe do? He puts his bottle down in the middle of the road and he says, "Present arms!" Up out of the bottle, swarming like ants, comes a whole army of little soldiers, and they run away from the bottle in all directions, springing up as they went until they was all six-feet tall, in bright red coats and carrying rifles. They formed up in squads, and the Captain of 'em all salutes and says, "What orders, sir?"

'Joe points at the town hall and he says, "Capture that!"

'So the bottle-soldiers marched on the town hall, and the guards no sooner sees 'em than they run away – and so would you if you seen soldiers come out of a beer bottle – and the soldiers march into the town hall, and secure it, and they drag out mayor Jack, and throw him down on his knees in front of Joe.

'Joe snatches the mayor's chain from round Jack's neck and says, "You lying two-faced back-stabbing good-for-nothing toe-rag, where's my half of the treasure? What d'you mean by leaving my wife and kids to go hungry and cold while you're prinking round here, dressing your missis up in diamonds? I trusted you. We was friends."

' "I'm sorry," says Jack. "I meant to give your wife her share. All the way here, I did, honest. But when it come to it, I couldn't help thinking how much more I could do with all of the treasure instead of half. Can you honestly say, Joe, that you wouldn't have done the same, if the boot had been on the other foot?"

' "Well, I dunno," says Joe. "I'd like to think I'd have

been honest, however much I was tempted, but maybe I'm kidding meself. All right," he says, "get up. So long as I get every penny that's owing to me, we'll say no more about it. But I'll tell you this – since you tried to cheat me, I shall be hanging on to the tablecloth."

' "That's fair," says Jack, and Joe says to the soldiers, "Back to barracks!" And they all run back to the bottle, shrinking as they went, until they'd all gone back inside it.

'Well, Jack handed over Joe's share of the treasure, and that made Joe a rich, rich man. He bought a new house, with plenty of room for hisself and his wife and all their children; and he had all his children educated, and they all et well, and had lots of clothes and shoes. It was a different life from the one they'd led!

'And every day, Joe invited the poor and homeless into his house, spread the tablecloth and asked for a feast, then let everybody eat as much as they liked. He went on and on doing that, and more folk come every day, until the tablecloth wore out. The cloth got thinner and thinner, and went into holes, and didn't work so well, magicking up pea soup when it had been asked for ice cream, or ginger beer when it had been asked for apple pie. Then it stopped working altogether – and that's why there's no such thing in the world these days.

'What about the bottle of soldiers? Well, it's a sad story, what happened to them. The bottle was standing on the table one day when Joe and his wife had a row – a silly row about whether there ought to be another row of beans planted in the garden, or some sweetpeas instead. They got proper worked up about it and, in the middle of the row, Joe snatched up the bottle and throwed it across the room – not at his wife. He just throwed it, in a temper. But the bottle hit the wall and smashed.

'And there's all these tiny little soldiers, lying about among the broken glass, some of 'em hurt. Joe comes over, all worried, trying not to tread on 'em. "Another bottle!" the tiny Captain squeaks at him. "Put we in another bottle – quick!"

'Joe's wife goes running and comes back with an empty beer bottle, and Joe starts scooping the soldiers up and trying to tip and pour and push 'em into the neck of the bottle. It's a fiddly job, with Joe's big fingers and all these tiny little soldiers, but it's going all right – until almost all the soldiers am in, and then maybe Joe gets a bit careless 'cos he thinks he's almost done the job. Anyroad, what happens is, he tries to jam a couple of the soldiers in at once, and they get stuck in the neck. One of 'em's the little Captain. Joe tries to poke 'em down, but between the tight fit of the bottle-neck and Joe's rough handling, the little Captain faints dead away, and there he is, drooping over the neck of the bottle.

' "Fetch me another bottle of beer," Joe says, and his wife brings him one, and Joe pours the beer over the Captain, to bring him round. But as he's pouring, the other little soldier that's jammed in the neck slips down into the bottle, and the Captain slips down inside with him, and all the beer pours down on top of 'em, and fills the bottle – and all the little soldiers drown in the beer afore Joe can pour it off and save 'em. So that was the end of them, and that's why there's no bottles of soldiers in the world today.

'And it's a sorrier world for it.

'There's many a time I've wished I had a magic tablecloth and a bottle of soldiers. A lot of things would have turned out very different if I had.

'But that's the end of that story. If you want any more of it, you must make it up yourself.'

'Shall I tell a story now?' asks Granny Shearing. 'Or am you tired of listening to stories?'

'No, tell one,' said Polly. 'I shall like to remember all these stories when I'm away from home.'

'Clean your ears out and listen then.' With the scissors that hung from her belt, Granny Shearing cut through the wool as she finished her darn, and then bundled wool and socks together in her lap.

'You'll have heard,' said Granny Shearing, 'about King Arthur, the great King Arthur, who ruled the Summer Lands of Britain and held his shield to guard us from all our enemies. Well, King Arthur had a son – oh, not Mordred, who everybody's heard of, who caused him all that trouble. No, the son I'm talking about was Arthur's youngest son. He was named Llacheu, and he was a good boy, and never give any trouble and was his daddy's favourite.

'Now, you know how it was at Arthur's court. Every day folk was coming in, asking the knights to come and save 'em from something or other – from dragons and wizards and giant fire-breathing cats, and nine-headed serpents and the Lord knows what else.

'This one evening, when all the knights and all the ladies was at their dinner, in comes this poor old man, and he hobbles up to the King's table, and he says, "A favour, King! I've walked miles, walked for weeks, until me feet bleed and me ribs poke through, to come and ask you this favour."

' "Ask away," says the King.

' "I've got a daughter, King," says the old man. "The only child left to me, and I love her more than me own life. But King, her's haunted, her's possessed, her's taken from me by seven evil spirits—"

' "Seven!" says the King. "What, all at once?"

' "Oh King!" says the old man. "Once my daughter was beautiful and loving. Now her's red-eyed and drooling and don't know me. I beg you, King, help me. Help me destroy these spirits and bring my daughter back."

'The King looked up and down the crowded tables in his hall. "You all heard him," he said. "Who's going to volunteer?"

'But nobody was keen. This one had a duel on with a Black Knight, and another one had to fight two Red Knights. And there was a few Green Knights and Blue Knights to be dealt with an' all. Somebody else had to battle a herd of man-eating horses, and a whole football team of knights was off after the Questing Beast. There was nobody, no one among all them knights, who wanted to help the old man and his daughter.

'Just as King Arthur was going to say he'd have to do it hisself, somebody pulled at his sleeve, and he looked round to see his son, Llacheu, who'd only just turned sixteen, and was as slim and pretty as a girl. "I'll go," says Llacheu. "I'll do it."

' "Sit down and eat your dinner," says the King, his father. "You're too young. You're not ready. I'll go meself."

' "But you've got the land to rule, father," says Llacheu. "You're busy enough already. Let me go. I'm old enough. It's about time I started going on quests and adventures. You did, at my age."

' "That was different," says the King. He couldn't bear thought of swords and axes chopping at his son's body, or of losing him. "In another year or two, maybe, you can start. Now go and finish your dinner. I've got to get ready for this quest."

'But Llacheu followed him from the table, saying, "In two years' time I shall be eighteen! That's too late to start – I shall be laughed at. Please let me go and help this old man, Father. Nobody else wants to go. I'll do it. I'll do a good job, I swear I will."

' "It's not that I don't think you'll do a good job," says the King. "It's too dangerous. Tricky things, evil spirits. You don't know what they might do. You haven't the experience. A nice, straightforward dragonet is what you want, to start on. Next time one comes up, I'll let you have it."

' "But when one does, you'll give it to somebody else," says Llacheu. "I know you, you'll have some excuse not to send me. I want to go on *this* quest, Father. Please let me. Please."

' "No," says the King. "And that's final."

' "You think I'm a coward," says Llacheu. "You think I

can't fight, but I can. I've been working hard. I'm ready. It's not fair."

' "It's not that I think you can't—" says the King.

' "Prove it, then," says Llacheu. "Let me go. I'm going to keep on until you let me, I'm not going to give you any peace. If you don't let me go, I'll never forget it – and I'll never let *you* forget it. I shall—" Well, you know how it goes. Llacheu kept on and on all the time his father was trying to get armed ready for the quest, until in the end, King Arthur said, "All right then, go! And if you come back dead I shall give you such a hiding!"

'So Llacheu was well pleased, and ran off to get his own armour and horse ready. And King Arthur had a pack-pony loaded with gold, so his son wouldn't be short of anything he needed.

'The old man, the lady's old dad, was going to travel with Llacheu, to guide him on the way, but Llacheu said, "No, Uncle, you're tired out, you'd only slow me down. You stay here in comfort, and let me deal with it all."

'So the old man told him the road he had to go, and stayed behind, and Llacheu set off, singing, in high spirits, riding his big horse, and leading the pack-pony loaded with treasure.

'Now Llacheu went by hill, he went by stream, he went by stone, he went by moor, he went longer and further than I've got words or breath to tell of, but in the end he come to a town, where he thought he might break his journey and give his horse a good rest and a feed. But as he was passing through the market-place, he found a great crowd

70

of people, all shouting and arguing. He pushed through the crowd with his horses, to find out what was going on and, in the middle of the crowd, a dead man was lying on the ground, with his shroud pulled away from his face. The people was all jostling round this dead body, and some of 'em stooped down and felt in the shroud, stripping the dead man naked, as if they was looking for something hidden in his wrappings.

'Well, young Llacheu, he's shocked. He's never seen anything like it. So he stands in his stirrups and shouts, "What's going on here? Why isn't this dead man buried, as he should be? Or at least lying in a chapel? Why is he out here on the ground, being squabbled over? It's like seeing a lot of kites flapping over the body of a dead dog."

'All the people in the crowd start shouting at once. It seemed the dead man died owing a lot of money to all the tradesmen in the town. "And he's not being buried until we get our money!"

' "That's easy settled," says Llacheu. "I have money. I shall pay this dead man's debts. I'll be staying in that inn over there. Let all who have bills to be paid come to me there, and I'll settle with them in full. But before I pay out a penny, I want this man properly coffined and buried."

' "I'm the undertaker," says a man in the crowd. "Who's going to pay for the funeral?"

' "I shall, of course," says Llacheu. "Present your bill along with all the others."

'Off he goes to the inn. He sees his horse and pack-pony

made comfortable in the stables, but he hasn't time to wash or eat hisself, because by the time he crosses the stable-yard to the inn, there's a great crowd of people waiting for him and a queue all down the street.

'Now there's honest folk in the crowd, who've got bills all properly made out: bills for drink, bills for food, bills for boots and coats and breeches and cloaks and hats; bills for horses and carriages and horse-feed; bills for chairs and tables and jewellery and paintings and swords – he must have lived in high old style, this dead man. Llacheu settles all them bills.

'And word gets round, and more folk come, from further away, with more bills. And there is them, who seeing that Llacheu's so young and girl-faced, think he's a fool and come to him with sob stories about how the dead man owed 'em a thousand pounds in gambling debts, or for apple trees for an orchard, or for trout to fill a lake. "Have you a signed bill?" says Llacheu. "If you have, I'll pay it. If you haven't, then goodbye."

' "Oh, but I never had a bill, it was a debt of honour." Or, "I had a bill, but I lost it – the dog ate it – my maid threw it away."

' "No bill, no payment," says Llacheu. "Look after your business affairs better."

'But even though he's canny like that, by the time he's paid all the dead man's debts, he's got just enough to settle his own bill at the inn, and then nothing left at all of the treasure his father give him to see him on his way. "Oh well," he thinks, "I shall just have to manage as best I can." He won't think of turning round and going home.

'Next morning, Llacheu's up early, while it's still dark, getting his horse and pony ready, by lantern-light, in the stable-yard. There comes up to him a man who says, "You're travelling?"

' "Aye," says Llacheu. "I've got far to go."

' "D'you want company on the road?" says the stranger.

' "Company is always good," says Llacheu, but he's not so sure he wants this man's company. In the lantern-light, the man's an ugly customer. His face is sort of grey, like he's very sick, and his eyes are sunken in and staring, and his mouth pulled back in a grin.

' "Then we'll travel together," says the man. "Maybe we can be a help to one another."

' "Maybe," says the prince. "My name's Llacheu ap Arthur. What's yours?"

' "Call me Lazarus," says the man. And they start on the road together.

'They travel all that day, and when the sun comes up, Lazarus looks even worse than he did by lantern-light. He hasn't got much to say for hisself neither but, late on, when the birds are starting to roost, he says, "It's time we found lodgings for the night."

' "I've got no money," says Llacheu, "so I'll be sleeping under hedge somewhere. But you go on and find lodgings, and we'll meet again in the morning."

' "I can't sleep warm and dry and let you sleep under a hedge," says Lazarus. "Tell you what: I know where we can both sleep for nothing. A little way down this road," he says, "there's a castle where lives a giant with three heads."

' "*Three* heads?" says Llacheu.

' "Three heads. One has a black beard, one a ginger beard, and one a blond beard. The black-bearded head eats like we: meat and fish and bread and fruit and all that. The ginger-bearded head eats nothing at all but vegetables and fruit. The blond-bearded head, though, that one's a cannibal. It eats men and women and children."

' "An interesting fellow," says Llacheu.

' "More than you know," says Lazarus. "He's a fierce fighter – why he's known to have overcome and killed five hundred men in armour. He sat amongst 'em on the battlefield, cracking open the suits of armour and eating the men inside – feeding 'em to his blond-bearded head – like a man cracking open crabs or lobsters."

' "He's certainly worth hearing about," says Llacheu, "but what has he got to do with finding lodgings?"

' "We'll lodge with him," says Lazarus.

' "What, are you mad?" says Llacheu. "After what you've just told me? The blond-bearded head will eat us – we won't even be a snack for him."

' "Don't worry about it," says Lazarus. "I'll go ahead and arrange our lodgings."

' "Don't be a fool, don't go," says Llacheu. "Look, here's a good spot to set up camp for the night. There's trees for shelter and a stream for water. We'll stay here and be on our road early in the morning."

' "Good idea," says Lazarus. "You set up camp and stop here, and I'll come back for you when I've made arrangements with the giant. Don't go away."

' "I wish you wouldn't go," said Llacheu. "It isn't safe or wise."

' "I'm a grown man," says Lazarus, "and can do as I please – just as you did when you left your father." And off went Lazarus down the road, leaving Llacheu with his mouth open, wondering how Lazarus knowed anything about him and his father.

'Down the road goes Lazarus until he gets to the giant's castle. Great big towers and walls against the sky. The ground round it is all scattered with bones – human bones – and they've been cracked to get the marrow. Lazarus picks his way through all the bones and goes up to the castle door and knocks with the big knocker. And the giant with three heads looks over the castle wall, and the black-bearded head shouts, "Who's knocking at my door?"

' "Just a little squirt of a man," says the red-bearded head, peering down.

' "Worth eating?" says the blond-bearded head, and takes a look. "No: there's more meat on a sparrow's leg."

' "You'd better listen to me," Lazarus shouts. "I've come to warn you and save your life!"

' "Huh!" says black beard. "What could threaten me?"

' "Haven't you heard of Llacheu ap Arthur, King Arthur's famous son?" says Lazarus. "Don't you know he's coming here to get you?"

' "Never heard of him," says red beard. "Why should we worry about him?"

' "Let him come," says blond beard. "I'll eat him."

' "He's coming with his army—" says Lazarus.

' "What do we care?" says red beard. "We can overcome and kill five hundred men."

' "But he has an army of more than a thousand men," says Lazarus. "Can you overcome a thousand armoured men?"

'The three heads look at one another, but they don't say nothing to that. They'm thinking, five hundred men, easy. Six hundred men, maybe. Seven hundred men, w-e-ll . . . But a *thousand*?

' "And Llacheu ap Arthur, he's worth five hundred men just by hisself," says Lazarus. "He's a giant – he's almost as big as you are – his neck's thicker than most folk's thighs – his shoulders am like mountains – he can lift cart-horses over his head, one in either hand. And what a face! He's got a face to frighten children – so many scars, it looks like a whetstone folk have sharpened their swords on. And he's coming after you!"

'The giant hunched up and ducked, so not so much of him showed over the castle wall as afore.

' "And what a temper he's got!" says Lazarus. "He's worth five hundred men when he's in a good mood. But when he gets mad! A fighting temper comes on him. You can tell when it does, 'cos his one eye shrinks down as small as a pin and his other eye swells up as big as a cartwheel. His body spins round and round like a top inside his skin with a whirring noise louder than a thousand screaming cats; and a fountain of blood a hundred feet high shoots up from the top of his head. And then he fights like a thousand men! And nothing that gets in his way survives. And he's coming to get you."

' "Oh dear oh," says the giant, and he shrinks down behind his castle wall.

' "He's coming here," says Lazarus, "in a terrible temper, with a thousand men, and he means to chop you into pieces small, and tear down your castle until not one stone stands on another — and then he's going to sow the land with salt so nothing'll ever live here again, not even a single blade of grass."

'The giant starts wailing and crying. "What shall we do?" says black-bearded head.

' "What can we do?" says red beard.

' "We can go down to our vault and lock ourselves in," says blond beard. "Pretend we're not in until he goes away. That's all we can do." And blond beard shouts out, "Hey, you down there! Are you on our side?"

' "I come and warned you, didn't I?" says Lazarus. "I could just have let the King's son chop you to pieces."

' "Do this for we, then," says blond beard. "Shut we in our vault and lock it after we, and keep the keys until this Llacheu ap Arthur's gone away."

' "Oh, I'll do that for you, be glad to," says Lazarus. So the giant hauls up his drawbridge and Lazarus goes in. The giant shows him a big underground stone vault at the bottom of one of the towers, and gives him the keys. Lazarus waits until the giant's gone into the vault, and then he locks all the seven big locks, and shoots the bolts, and puts the bars across, so there's no chance of the giant getting out.

'Next thing, Lazarus hunts round the castle and finds out all the giant's servants, who were hiding from the giant, afraid they might be eaten if the blond-bearded head noticed them. "Listen here," says Lazarus. "I've got rid of the giant for you, so I want you to do as I say. I'm going to fetch my friend now and, when we get back, I want the stables ready for our horses, and I want a good fire burning in a comfortable room, and a good meal; and then I want hot water for baths, and comfortable beds. And we shall want breakfasts in the morning." And all the servants, grateful for being rid of the giant, hurry off to carry out his orders.

'Off Lazarus goes, back to where he left Llacheu and says, "All right, come on, the giant's not at home. We can make weselves comfortable in his castle and never give him a thought."

' "Are you sure?" Llacheu says.

' "I tell you it's safe," says Lazarus. "Are you a man or a little boy? Now come on."

'So Llacheu goes with him to the castle, and servants come out to meet 'em and take their horses, and other servants lead 'em into a warm, comfortable room with a big fire burning in the hearth. The table's spread with every kind of food, hot and cold, that they could fancy, and when they've eaten so much that they're tired out with eating, the servants come in and say, "Your baths are ready." And when they've bathed, their beds are ready, and Llacheu falls into the comfortable bed and sleeps like the dead.

'And all this while, the giant with three heads is locked in his vault, shivering with cold, hungry, thirsty and getting no sleep.

'Next morning, Lazarus is up while it's still dark, and with the giant's keys he opens the castle treasury, and loads the pack-pony up with more treasure. He gets the horses ready in the yard, and goes inside to find Llacheu eating his breakfast. "Hurry up and finish that and be on your way," he says.

' "Aren't you coming?" says Llacheu.

' "I'll catch you up," says Lazarus. "I got things to do here."

' "Well, if we don't see each other again, good luck go with you," says Llacheu. "You've been a good friend to me."

'When Llacheu's out of sight, Lazarus goes down to the door of the vault and knocks on it. "It's me," he calls out to the giant inside. "Llacheu ap Arthur's furious that he can't find you. He's going to tear your castle apart stone from stone anyway. But I think I could talk him out of it – if you made it worth my while."

' "There's gold and jewels in the treasury," the black-bearded head whispers back. "Help yourself to all you want."

' "No good," says Lazarus. "Llacheu ap Arthur's already emptied the treasury. You'll have to pay me with something else."

' "Go up to our bedchamber," says red beard, "and hanging on the bedpost you'll find a ragged old coat."

' "You insult me," says Lazarus. "What do I want with a raggedy old coat?"

' "It's magic," says blond beard. "When you put it on, it makes you invisible."

' "Oh," says Lazarus. "Don't go away. I'll go and give it a try."

'He runs up to the giant's bedchamber and there's this raggedy old coat hanging on the bedpost. On the wall there's a spotty mirror, and while he's looking in the mirror, he puts the coat on, and watches hisself disappear. "Very good," he says, and putting the coat over his arm, he goes back down to the vault.

' "I've had a word with Llacheu ap Arthur," he says, "but I only made him mad. He's determined to pull your castle down."

' "Talk to him again," says red beard. "We don't want to lose our castle."

' "I'd be risking my own life to say another word to him about it," says Lazarus. "You'll have to pay me something more if you want me to do that."

' "Go and look on the hatstand by the front door," says blond beard. "You'll find a tweed cap. Have that."

' "You offer me a tweed cap to risk my life?" says Lazarus. "It'll take more than that."

' "This tweed cap is a Cap of Knowledge," says black beard. "Put it on your head and you'll know all that you need to know."

' "Oh, right-o," says Lazarus. "I'll just go and give it a try."

Off he goes, and finds the hatstand and the tweed cap, and he puts on the cap. Straightaway, he knows all kinds of things: so many things it's no good me trying to tell you the half of it. "Very good," he says, and puts the cap with the raggedy coat.

'Back he goes to the vault. "Llacheu ap Arthur started spinning in his skin when I brought the subject up again," he says, "but I think he's starting to listen. I want some better payment, though, afore I say another word."

' "This is blackmail," says blond beard. "We've paid you enough already."

' "Fair enough," says Lazarus. "I'll just stand by and let Llacheu ap Arthur pull your castle down round your ears, shall I? And when he breaks up the vault, he'll find you, and a fountain of blood'll spring from his head, and his one eye'll grow small and his other eye'll grow huge, and he'll spin round inside his skin, and chop you into pieces small. That's what you want, is it?"

' "Oh, all right," says black beard. "Go to the cupboard under the stairs in the north tower, and you'll find a pair of old brown boots – afore you complain," he says, "they're seven-league boots. Put 'em on, and they'll carry you seven leagues with every stride."

' "Not bad," says Lazarus, "but come on. If I'm to talk Llacheu ap Arthur round, I need something really *good*."

' "Then go to the chapel," says red beard. "Look behind the altar, and you'll find a rusty sword."

' "A rusty old sword?" says Lazarus.

' "Whatever you strike with that sword will be cut in

two," says blond beard, "even if it's made of stone or iron."

' "Right you are," says Lazarus, and he goes and finds the boots and the sword. He sits down and has a snack, and then puts on the raggedy old coat, that makes him invisible, and picks up the rusty old sword, and goes back to the vault. "I've talked and I've talked until me jaw aches," he says, "and I've talked Llacheu ap Arthur into going away. I've saved your castle. So now I'm going to let you out." And he lifts up the bar, pulls back all the bolts, and unlocks all the seven locks.

'Out comes the giant, rubbing the eyes in all his three heads, after being in the dark, and stretching his arms and back after being cramped up in the vault. He don't see Lazarus, 'cos Lazarus is wearing the coat that makes him invisible. And Lazarus takes the rusty sword and snick! cuts the giant right in two. That's the end of him.

'All the castle servants are so grateful to Lazarus for killing the giant for 'em, they want him to stay while they give him a feast. They want him to be the lord of the castle. But Lazarus says, "Sorry. I've got to catch up with my friend." And off he goes, hurrying along the road, to find Llacheu.

'Well, he found him, and Llacheu's glad to see him again, because even if Lazarus is a sickly, ugly-looking sort of cove, Llacheu's come to like him. And they travel on together, by stream and stone, by hill and dale, longer and further than I've got breath or time to tell you, until they get to the big house where lives the lady possessed by seven evil spirits.

'They knock at the door, and servants let 'em in, and take their horses, and when Llacheu says he's come to see their mistress, they look worried, but tell him to wait, and they'll tell her. So Llacheu and Lazarus wait in this big room, by a fire, and by and by the door opens and in comes the lady. Her hair's all tangled and greasy and knotted and hangs down round her shoulders and over her face; and her eyes peer through it, all narrow and shining red, like the eyes of a fierce pig peering through a thicket. Her frock's hanging off her shoulders, and it's all torn and smeared with mud and blood and food, and her comes across the room all hunched up, prowling like an animal. Now, our Llacheu's no coward, but it's all he can do to keep hisself from running away.

'The lady comes right up to him, and the smell of her near knocks him over. "Have you come to see me?" her says, and holds out her hand to him. Her hands are all grimy, with long, long nails; and there's all dirt under the nails, and dirt and mud round the rings on her fingers, like her'd been digging in the earth.

'Llacheu steels hisself, and he takes her hand, and bows over it and kisses it, like he would with any lady. "I've come to help you," he says.

'Her leaves her hand in his, and bridles and lifts up her hair, so they can see how dirty her face is; and her smirks and says, "Have you come courting me, pretty man?"

'Llacheu doesn't want to answer that, so he bows over her hand again, and says, "To help you, Lady."

' "How kind of you," her says, and rings a bell. In come seven servants, all dressed in black, and an ugly, scabby looking crew they are too. "Prepare beds for my guests," her says, "and set a table for 'em."

'The servants turn round to go, and Llacheu catches a glimpse of a tail hanging out of the breeches of one, and a funny shaped shoe on the foot of another, and a horn peeping out of the hair of the head on a third – so he's in no doubt as to who these seven servants am.

'In no time – like magic – a table's set with food and drink, and Lazarus and Llacheu are sitting down with the lady, eating and drinking while one of the seven servants plays music. The lady never stops flirting with Llacheu. Her's rubbing his foot and leg with hers under the table, and feeding him bits of dainties off her fork, and making kissing mouths at him and winking – and while her's doing all this, the snot runs down from her nose, through the grime on her face and into her mouth along with her food. And her wipes it off with her dirty fingers, and then reaches across the table to take Llacheu's hand in hers. He can hardly bear to look at her, but he won't be rude. He takes her hand and holds it. He feels sorry for her.

'Right at the end of the evening, when they've eaten and drunk all they want – or all they can stomach – the lady pulls handkerchief out of the bodice of her dress. It's all grubby and stained with something. Leaning across the table, her wipes Llacheu's mouth with it, and he holds still and lets her. Then her waves the handkerchief in his face and says, "Tomorrow morning you must give me this handkerchief again. If you don't, my servants will cut off your head." Saying that, her stuffs the handkerchief back down her frock, gets up and goes out of the room, laughing.

' "How can I show her that handkerchief tomorrow morning?" says Llacheu. "I don't know where her sleeps – if her sleeps – and even if I did, how can I take the handkerchief off her? Poor woman. The evil spirits have made her mad – I can't take advantage of her, and I can't take it from her by force. It wouldn't be right."

'A couple of the servants in black come in, bowing and grinning and saying, "Can we show you to your bedchambers, sirs?"

' "Go to your room and sleep, if you can," says Lazarus. "Maybe some good idea will come to us in the night."

'So they go to their rooms, which are clean and comfortable, with fires burning in the hearth. But Llacheu gets no sleep. He sits up by the fire all night, wracking his brains for some way of getting the handkerchief without doing the lady any wrong.

'Lazarus don't waste no time. He puts on the tweed cap, and right away he knows what he needs to know. He puts on the raggedy old coat of invisibility, and tucks the seven-league boots under his arm, and he sneaks through the corridors to the room where the lady sleeps – the cap told him where it is. Quietly, he opens the door, and slides inside while her ain't looking. The lady's sitting by her bedroom fire, combing her tangled hair with her long nails. Lazarus just leans against the wall and watches her. Her can't see him.

'At midnight, in come the seven servants, but now they've

got no clothes on, and their horns and cloven-hoofed feet and long spiky tails are plain to see. "Oh, you've come, you've come," says the lady, jumping up and spreading her arms. "Take me away, take me to my love, take me to the fires!"

'The seven servants crowd round her and catch her by the arms and spin her round, and spin her away into the air – and Lazarus pulls on his boots fast. He lunges after 'em, and catches the tail of the last servant, and he runs after 'em through the air in great seven-league strides. The servant squeals at the pull on his tail, but all the others are shrieking and howling an' all, and the lady's laughing, so nobody takes any notice.

'The servants carry the lady right into Hell, where it's dark as pitch, but shot through with red glare from the fires; and the great halls of Hell ring and resound with screams and hollers and moans – a terrible place to be. And there's the devil hisself, with a great stand of antlers on his head, like a royal stag, and he takes the lady in his arms, and they dance among the fires and screams. They dance all night, but when morning's near, the lady pulls the handkerchief from the front of her frock and gives it to the devil. "Keep this," her says. "When I go back, I shall ask the boy for it, and when he can't give it to me, my seven servants'll cut off his head, and chop him into pieces small, and scatter his pieces over the earth – and King Arthur won't even have a grave whereby to mourn his son."

'The devil laughs, sounding like a stag booming, and he

takes the handkerchief and hangs it from the topmost prong of his antlers – and then the lady's servants gather round her and whirl her away through the air, away from Hell and back to earth and her home.

'But Lazarus is still in Hell, wearing his coat of invisibility. He sneaks up close to the devil, and jumps, and the magic boots give him a spring upwards – and he snatches the handkerchief from the devil's antlers. Then in great jumps and leaps, he travels back from Hell to earth, and goes to the room where Llacheu's sitting, fretful, by the fire.

' "Here's the hankie," he says. "It's morning. Go down to breakfast and show it to the lady."

'Llacheu jumps up and hugs Lazarus. "Thank you, thank you!" he says. "You've saved my life! How did you get it?"

' "We've got no time for gossiping," says Lazarus. "Be on your way."

'They go down together, and the lady's waiting for 'em, red eyes glaring through her hair, sniggering to herself. Behind her stand her seven servants.

"Here's the handkerchief you asked me to keep for you," says Llacheu, and holds it out to the lady. That stops her sniggering, and the seven servants all fall back, looking disappointed.

' "Come and sit by me and talk," says the lady, and all that day, her makes up to Llacheu. Her walks round the house with him, holds his hand, and snuggles up to him and leans against him. When they'm inside by the fire, her sits on his lap, and asks him if he likes her – and so on and so on, and through it all, Llacheu tries hard to be kind and polite, even though the lady stinks and has mad, red eyes, and he really wants her nowhere near him.

'That night the servants spread another feast, and the lady and Llacheu and Lazarus all sit down to it. The lady keeps on flirting with Llacheu, until right at the end of the evening, when her gets up to go to her bed, her leans down and kisses him on the lips – her own lips all wet with spit and snot.

' "Tomorrow morning," her says, "you must show me the lips that last I kissed, or my servants will cut off your head."

'Llacheu makes hisself smile and he says, "Kiss none but me, lady, and that will be easy." But when the lady's gone, he says to Lazarus, "How can I be sure she kisses no one but me?"

' "Go to your room," says Lazarus, "and sleep if you can." But Lazarus, he puts on his cap, and then he knows just what to do. He straps on his rusty sword, puts on his coat of invisibility, tucks his seven-league boots under his arm, and sneaks off to the lady's room, like before.

'The lady's seven servants come and carry her away to Hell, and Lazarus puts on his boots and follows. He stands invisible among all the fires and screams, and he watches the lady and the devil. The lady won't dance with the devil at first. Her's angry with him.

' "You wanted to see the boy's head, did you?" her says. "If you'd looked after the handkerchief, I'd have brought it with me. But he had the handkerchief, so he won the game!"

' "But you'll have played another game with him," says the devil.

'The lady laughed and went into the devil's arms, and as he ducked down his head, she kissed his lips and says, "If he can't show me your lips tomorrow morning, then I take his head. And I'll bring it to you tomorrow night."

'Lazarus stands, invisible, and watches 'em dance and play, until it's near morning, and the seven servants come and carry the lady away again. Then he goes up close to devil, draws his rusty sword and snick! chops off the devil's head. He carries it away by the antlers, carries it back to the lady's house, and the room where Llacheu's sleeping on the bed, still dressed. He was so tired he just fell asleep in his clothes.

' "Wake up," says Lazarus. "Dawn's here. The lady'll be asking to see the lips her kissed last – here they be." And he holds up the devil's head by the antlers.

'Llacheu's too surprised to speak – but then there's a knock at the door. Lazarus puts the devil's head down by the side of the bed, out of sight, just as the door opens and the lady comes in, with her seven servants behind her. Her red eyes shine through her tangles of hair, and her crawls onto the bed in her torn, dirty frock.

' "I couldn't wait to see you," her says. "Show me the lips I kissed last."

' "Here they be," says Llacheu, and he lifts up the devil's head by its antlers and holds it before her face.

'The lady wailed, and clapped her hands to her face, and squirmed away as if he'd chucked scalding water over her. And all the seven servants set up such a howling and a chow-rowing, such a hell-squealing, that Llacheu had to cover his ears and hold his head on.

'A wind blew, a great storm-wind, right inside the room. It roared, it banged on their ears: the kind of wind you can't stand up in. Llacheu held on to the bed, to keep from being blown into the air, and it shook under him, rattling. The hell-wind, it was, blowing the devils back to Hell. It blew and it sucked until the very stones of the walls moved with a din like grinding mill-stones. Lightning flashed, white. Thunder boomed, thunder crashed.

'The quiet, when it stopped, was deep as a feather-bed. It took a while afore Llacheu could believe he was still alive and in one piece. Then he looks up and looks round. The floor is all folded up and splintered. There's big cracks in the walls, and he can see the morning coming through 'em, and feel the breeze blowing.

'Lazarus is clinging to the bed-post by Llacheu's head, and gives him a grin. Llacheu's glad to see his friend hasn't been snatched away to Hell, or just blowed out through a hole in a wall. And then Llacheu sits up and looks round for the lady.

'Her'd been tumbled by the wind into a corner, and was just picking herself up and sorting herself out. Her pushes back her dirty hair, looks down at her torn frock and her long, dirty nails and says, "Why am I like this?" Her looks at Llacheu and Lazarus and the red light's gone out of her eyes, and all the ratty meanness out of her face. Her looks like a little girl who's been running wild in the fields, until her's all mucky and mussy. Her says, "Who am you? Why am you here?'

' "Lady," says Llacheu, "don't be afraid." He's pulling bits of mattress-straw and pillow-feather out of his hair. "I'm Llacheu ap Arthur ap Uther, Pendragon," he says. "And this is my friend and helper, Lazarus. We mean you no harm. We came to set you free."

' "I must wash," says the lady, jumping up. "I must change my clothes—" And out of the room her dashes, never noticing that the door's hanging off its hinges in tatters.

'When they see her next, her looks as different as a rose from a dung-heap. Her's put on clean clothes, and her hair's all smooth and shining. Her stands in the wreck of her hall and says, "I'm sorry the house is in such a state, and I don't seem to have anything in the larder to offer you—"

' "Lady," says Llacheu, "you mustn't worry about that."

' "And I haven't even said, thank you," her says, "for saving me from them seven evil spirits. What am I thinking of?"

' "Lady, never think of it again," says Llacheu. "Your father is waiting at my father's court for news of you. I think it best if you joined him, and I would be happy to escort you there."

' "I should like that," her says. "Can we go now?"

'So they all three travel back to King Arthur's court, and by the time they get there, Llacheu and the lady are in love, and they ask the lady's father if they can marry. He says yes – is he going to say no to King Arthur's favourite son? – and there's a big court wedding, with a whole week of feasting and dancing and music.

'The feasting's nearly over when Llacheu catches sight of his friend Lazarus standing in a dark corner; and he goes over to him and says, "My good friend, you stayed at my side, and gave me every help. I couldn't have won through without you. Please tell me what reward I can give you – if it's within my power to give, you shall have it."

' "Llacheu," says Lazarus, "you owe me nothing. I travelled with you, and helped you, to pay off the debt I owe *you*. Now we are square. Neither one owes the other anything at all."

' "What debt do you owe me?" Llacheu says.

' "Don't you remember," says Lazarus, "how you buried the dead man and paid off his debts?"

' "What has that to do with anything?" says Llacheu.

' "Everything," says Lazarus. "Goobye now. You'll never see me again. I'm going to lie down and sleep for ever in that quiet grave you bought me." And Lazarus walks out of the bright noisy feast hall and away into the dark.

'And so shall we all go to our graves, when our time comes. May they all be as peaceful.'

And Granny Shearing, finishing another darn, snips through another thread.

Three

Funeral Food

Old Peter, in his coffin, was carried away from his house on the shoulders of six men. His widow followed behind, with her sons and daughters, and their families. The sun shone. Flowers swayed among the thick greenery of the hedges. Birds called and whistled from the trees.

Three neighbours stayed behind at Peter's house, to make ready the food and brew the tea for when the mourners returned. Sunlight angling through the kitchen window gleamed on the thin edge of a milk jug and shone dully on the iron base of a pan hanging from a hook.

A long carving knife flashed in Granny Shearing's hand as she cut slices of bread and piled them on a white platter, while brown crumbs scattered on the cloth. At the table's other end, the cloth was folded back, to show the scrubbed wood, and there Clo was working, weaving strips of dough into little plaited loaves, to be sprinkled with black poppy seeds and baked. Letty counted the plates, cups and glasses, to be sure there were enough.

'I remember,' said Granny Shearing, 'when my mother's

second cousin died. A lot of folk went along to her lykewake – that's where the body's laid out, and folk light candles round it and sit up all night, watching. There was a couple of young lasses, Katie and Mary, among them that went. They'd never been to a lykewake afore. Didn't know what to expect.

'Well, the dead woman's family had got a couple of proper layers-out to come in and see to the body – they'd laid out scores of bodies, these two. Didn't bother 'em at all. They just stripped off the dead woman's clothes, tugging 'em off, letting everybody see the poor old thing's naked, stringy old arms and legs, and her bony old bare bum, and everything. They tossed the body here and heaved it there, and handled it like a lump of butcher's meat.

'These two young lasses, Katie and Mary, was shocked. They'd knowed the old woman when her'd been alive and walking about a couple of days afore, and when they see these layers-out washing her body down like it was a kitchen floor, and chatting about how much they was going to be paid and what they was going to get for their husband's dinner the next day – well, it made 'em shudder. They thought it wasn't right.

'They talked about it a lot. "I don't like to think," Katie says, "that when I die somebody'll lay me out like that. As if I didn't matter anymore – as if I'd never mattered."

' "When I die," says Mary, "I want somebody as cared about me to do what has to be done – to do it gentle-like."

' "With a bit of fondness," says Katie.

' "And not gossiping all the time."

' "With maybe a prayer being said," says Katie.

' "Tell you what," says Mary. "If I die afore you, I'd like you to lay me out, properly, like a friend, like you'd know I'd want it done."

' "I'll do it, I promise," says Katie. "And you promise that you'll do it for me if I die first." And Mary promised an' all.

'Well, time goes on, like it always does. The lasses got older, and they got married. Mary married a cobbler and lived in Daw End – in that little road just by the church. You know it.

'Katie married a farmer and went to live on his farm up on Hailstone Hill. It was one of them real old kind of farmhouses, where you had a passage through the middle of the house, from front to back, and at one side of the passage the people lived, and on the other side was the cattle-byre. It was a bit lonely, up there on the hillside, and Katie had never worked so hard in her life – within a year of the wedding, her'd got a little wench to look after, on top of all the farm-work – but still, her was happy. Her was so busy, her hadn't got time to be unhappy. Didn't see much of her old friends, though, not even Mary, who'd been her best friend.

'Anyroad, the May Day Fair come round, and Katie's husband had some cattle to sell, so he'd gone off to the fair and took their farm-man with him. And Katie said that the maidservant could go to the fair an' all, cos her was a good girl, and worked hard. "Go and enjoy yourself while you can, while you'm young and free," Katie says to her. So the upshot was, Katie was at the farm all by herself for a day and a night, except for the babby. But her was expecting her husband, and his man, and the maid back that day.

'At that time there was lots of beggars who used to tramp round from farm to farm, offering to do a bit of work or tell a fortune – anything for a bit of money, or something to eat, or a place to sleep. And this old beggar-woman turns up at the farm. Katie knows her from other times, and her's feeling a bit lonely, so her asks the old woman into the kitchen, and while Katie gets on with her chores, the old woman sits by the fire and tells her all the gossip.

' "You know the cobbler's wife in Daw End?" her says.

' "I know her very well!" says Katie. "Her's a good friend of mine. How is her?"

' "Oh, my dear, I'm so sorry I've got to give you the news," says the old beggar-woman. "You knowed her was in the family way?"

' "I knowed that," Katie says, and her starts to feel cold, the way you do when you guess the worse and know you'm going to be told it's true.

' "Oh my dear, the news hasn't got out here yet," says the old beggar-woman. "Her died last night. Her and the babby both. The babby killed her."

' "Oh no," Katie says, and sits down. "Oh no, oh no."

'The old beggar-woman took herself off soon after, not wanting to hang around where her'd had to deliver such bad news.

'Katie thought of strangers laying Mary out, stripping her and mauling her about and not caring a bit about her, and her wanted to put on her shawl and bonnet and start out for Daw End right then and there. But, 'course, her couldn't. It was a long road to carry a babby, and there was nobody at home to leave the babby with. And her couldn't go away and leave the farm empty with nobody there at all, for fear a coal should fall out of the fire and catch the hearth-rug – and if her put the fire out, then her husband would come home to a cold house and nothing to eat . . .

'Her kept jumping up, determined to go and then, when her had her bonnet on, her'd see that her just couldn't, and her'd take it off again. Her kept going outside, to look across the fields and down the lane, to see if her could see her husband coming home. Once they come, her kept telling herself, I'll be off down Daw End fast as I can.

'It was late on in the afternoon, and the light was going. Soon it'd be too dark to go to Daw End, but Katie still kept going out into the yard to look across the fields. And then her sees the maid coming home – dressed all in white and coming across the meadow in the evening sun. Every little ridge and hollow in the field's lit up or marked in shadow, and this woman in white comes picking her way over 'em all, coming on towards the farmhouse.

'Good, Katie thinks. As soon as her gets here, I'll leave her to look after the babby, and I'll get off to Daw End. And her goes back into the house, to do as much as her can towards getting her husband's dinner ready afore her has to go and leave it to the maid. After a bit, her has another look out of the window, and there's the maid, in her long white frock, still coming on. Her's nearer now; her'll be at the house afore long.

'The babby's lying in her cradle by the fire, and Katie picks her up, and sits down with her in one of the chairs by the hearth. Her thinks her'll give the babby a cuddle while her's waiting for the maid to come the last little bit of the way. While her's sitting there, tickling the babby, her hears the cattle in the byre start to stamp their feet and snort and jostle, so her knows that the maid's reached the house and is going along by the byre towards the door – that's what disturbing the cattle, see. So Katie looks up at the door, to see the maid come in. "I'm glad you've come," her says.

'At the door's a tall figure wrapped all in white. Even the head's wrapped up. It ain't a frock it's wearing. It's a shroud.

'Katie's heart near fell out of her. Her sat and watched the thing walk in at the door, and her hugged the babby so hard, it started to whimper. Across the floor to the hearth comes the thing, and sits itself down just across from Katie, in the other chair. Then two blue-white, dead-white arms come out of the shroud and lift hands up towards the wrappings round its head. It pulls at the wrappings, and pulls at 'em, and away they come to show its face – all dead white, and dead eyes, and it's glaring and glowering at Katie.

'Katie sat in her chair with the babby in her lap, and her couldn't move. The thing was between her and the door, and not for anything would her have gone one step closer to it.

'It kept staring at her, and her wanted to say, "I didn't

mean to break me promise. I'd have come if I'd knowed. I'd have come if I could." Her didn't say any of it. Her was scared that if her spoke, the thing would answer her, and her didn't want to hear its voice, or anything it might say.

'And it sits there, this thing that was her friend, scowling and waiting. Waiting for her to move, or to speak – 'cos a ghost can't speak until it's spoken to.

'The worst of it is, it's getting dark. The afternoon light's fading away outside, and inside the little kitchen it gets gloomier and gloomier. Katie ain't had chance to light any candles, so the only light is from the fire, and the fire's dying. The room gets colder, and the light comes closer and closer to the fire as it goes out, leaving the corners of the room all dark.

'Katie's getting frantic. The fire'll go out, and the last of the daylight'll go, and then her'll be in the dark with this thing. And in the dark, when her can't hardly see it, it'll get up from its chair and . . .

'Her's so scared, her moves at last. Her reaches out her arm to the babby's cradle, and her snatches up a big handful of the straw that lines it. Her throws the straw into the fire – but it's so light that some of it floats in the air and drifts to the floor and onto the hem of the shroud.

'But most of it goes into the grate, and the last of the red embers catch it, and it flares up and throws a bright yellow light round the room. It lights the dead woman up as her sits there, waiting, her shroud all in folds around her.

'But, 'course, straw don't burn for long. Soon as it's flared up, it's gone, and the room's darker than afore. Katie snatches up another handful of straw and throws that at the fire an' all. Some of it goes drifting round in the air, and lands on the ghost and in Katie's own hair – but what does go in the fire gives another few seconds of bright light so Katie can see the thing watching her across the hearth.

'There ain't much straw left in the cradle now. Katie throws a smaller handful into the fire, but it burns up so fast it gives hardly any light at all. And when it goes out, the room's so dark that all her can see of the thing in the chair is the greyish blur of its shroud in the mirk. Her thinks her sees it lean forward and press its hands on the arms of the chair, as if to get up.

'So her grabs that last bit of straw and chucks it on the fire. The light flares up, and the ghost sits back in its chair – but that's the last bit of straw there is.

'And then her husband shouts from outside. "Kates! We'm home, Kates!"

' "In here!" her shouts. "In here!" Oh, her feels all weak and watery with thankfulness, and falls back in the chair. Her's all but fainting when her husband comes in.

' "What you sitting in the dark for?" he says, and he lights candles at the fire. And the chair on the other side of the hearth's empty. "What's up?" her husband says. "You look a bit moithered."

'Her tries to tell him, but he just says, "You dozed off and dreamed it, silly lass."

'Well, the place is so cheerful with the candles lit, and her husband and the maid and the man all home again, that her thinks maybe her did dream it. And after her's had summat to ate, her feels a lot better.

' "But I ought to go over to Daw End and see what I can do," her says.

' "Not tonight," her husband says. "Leave it till the morning and I'll take you over there."

'So the next morning, her gets up behind her husband on his hoss, and he rides her over to Daw End, and her finds that Mary is dead, so her hadn't dreamed that part. And when her goes into the house, Mary's already been laid out on the kitchen table and wrapped in her shroud. And caught in the shroud are little wisps of straw – the little wisps that drifted about when Katie was throwing the straw into the fire.

'Katie never was the same after that.

'I should think not!' Letty said. 'What you want to tell horrible story like that for?'

'It's true,' said Granny Shearing.

'As true as I'm standing here in a diamond tiara and a cloth of gold frock,' Letty said. 'You want to hear a true ghost story? I'll tell you a true ghost story. Listen.'

'This happened out at Bilbrook,' Letty said. 'A friend of mine knowed the old couple.

'Well, this old couple, they lived in a little cottage at the edge of the common, where they grazed a couple of goats. They'd dug over a bit of land to grow some vegetables, but they couldn't manage much. It was hard life. They only just got by.

'They had the one son – they'd had other children, but

101

they'd died. You might have expected this son to help his mam and dad out a bit, but when he was sixteen, he took hisself off. They never seen him again after that, never got a word or a letter, nothing. They didn't know if he was alive or dead.

'They went on living in their cottage, the old folk, managing as well as they could. But the cottage got more and more ramshackle, letting in the wind and rain – 'cos they couldn't keep it in repair. And keeping the goats and keeping up the vegetable patch was getting harder for 'em. Neighbours seen they was getting thinner.

'But, next thing, the neighbours see that the goats was outside the cottage, bleating to be milked. And when they went up and knocked on the door, the cottage was empty. The old folk have upped and gone, left the goats to fend for theirselves and the cottage to fall down.

'First off, nobody knowed where the old couple had gone, but gossip started saying they'd come into money and moved away to town. Nobody believed it for a bit. Where would the money have come from, and why would the couple have taken off so sudden without a word to anybody? But then the carter, who went into town regular, said he'd seen 'em, and they was better dressed than he'd ever knowed 'em.

' "All silk hats and lace and furbelows," he said. "All scrubbed faces and polished boots. You could hear the money jingling from across the street."

'Well, as a rule a thing like that's all the talk for a week or so, but then it's forgot. The old couple wasn't forgot, though.

That's because folk who passed their old cottage at night seen lights flickering inside, and heard noises like somebody throwing crockery about. Folk stopped going round that way after dark.

'But there was this cottage standing empty, and you know somebody's going to move into it. They soon moved out again. There was no peace under that roof. Somebody that nobody could see walked round and round it all night long. Somebody that nobody could see opened doors and windows and stood at the side of beds and groaned.

'After that, the cottage stood empty for years. But then this family of tinkers moved in. It was the tinker's wife's idea. Her'd had enough of tramping the roads and sleeping in fields and her wanted house. "Its roof's off, and its windows are out," her said. "It ain't much better than an open field – but all it takes is work. We can make it a right warm, dry little cottage." And when folk warned her about it being haunted, her just said, "This is my door, and my roof and my hearth now, and it'll take more than a ghost to drive me out of it."

'The ghost near won, though, for all that. Soon as it got dark they heard footsteps wandering round the cottage and up and down the stairs. There was hammering on the walls, and doors and windows opened even when the doors and windows weren't there any more. Cups and plates and tools was moved about, and worse of all was this sighing and groaning they kept hearing. It sounded like a man, a sick and sorry man, but there was nothing to see.

'The tinker soon wanted to leave, but his wife wouldn't

budge. "Where will we find a better place than this?" her said. "No rent, and a vegetable patch, and the common to graze animals on. I'll be a ghost meself afore I leave."

'Instead, her come into the village and started asking about for somebody who knowed how to lay a ghost. Her didn't find anybody, but word went round, the way it does, and the next thing, the vicar's wife come to visit the tinkers. "I think I can lay your ghost," her says.

' "How much?" says the tinker's wife, who was a blunt sort of woman.

' "I ain't going to charge you nothing!" says vicar's wife. "I see it as my duty, to set a poor disturbed soul free, and to help you out as well. But what I got to ask you to do is to clear out for tonight and leave the house to me. Don't come back till full light. I don't want any interruptions."

' "That's easy enough," says the tinker's wife. "We've slept out often enough afore. But will you be all right?"

' "Oh, don't worry about me," says vicar's wife. "I know what I'm doing. I shall have a Bible in my hand, and God's hand over me."

'So, in the afternoon, tinker and his wife sets up a camp in a little thicket of trees not far from the cottage, and just as it's getting dark, they take their children off to it, and leave the vicar's wife on her own.

'Her sits her down by the fire, with the Bible in her lap, and her's got a bit of knitting with her, to pass away the time. Soon as it's full-dark, the footsteps start, up and down the poky little stairs. Doors open and close, and vicar's wife knows there's nobody in the house but her, and half the doors am off their hinges anyroad. Her ain't feared. Her says a quiet prayer to herself and keeps on sewing.

'It gets later – it's getting on for midnight – and her starts to get that feeling you get when somebody's standing right close to you – so close you can almost feel their shadow touching you. And her hears, right by her, a long, groaning sigh – but there's nobody there.

'A bit of a grue goes through her at that. It takes her a minute to find her voice, but her puts her two hands flat on the Bible and her says, "If you've summat to say to me, come to me and say it."

'Just then, her hears the sound of the church clock striking midnight across the fields. And the door of the cottage slams open and in comes – snorting and slathering – a great big stinking black pig, with great tusks, and snot dripping from its mouth and nose, and hot, hot breath.

' "In God's name," calls out vicar's wife, "if ever you were a Christian spirit, come to me in your own shape!" And the pig's shape sort of shrinks and dwindles away, and grows up tall and thin, and there's a young man standing there, with long hair and a thick black beard and skin very tanned.

' "In God's name I command you," says the vicar's wife, "to speak the truth and tell me why you haunt this place."

' "Oh thank God, thank God," says the ghost, "at last I can speak. Do you know the old couple who used to live here, in this cottage?"

' "I remember 'em," says the vicar's wife. "I think they'm

still alive, in town – 'least, I haven't heard that either of 'em's died."

' "I am, I was, their only son," says the ghost. "I ran away from home when I was sixteen – a long time ago."

' "I heard some talk of it," says the vicar's wife.

' "I was sick of living here, with nothing," says the ghost. "Of living in this hovel, with a couple of scrubby goats and a few rows of carrots. I had plans to make myself a rich man."

' "And did you?" says the vicar's wife.

' "I went to Australia, and I dug for gold and opals. Luck was with me, and I worked hard an' all. When I come back to England, I was a rich man. I could have come home in a silk suit, driving a motor-car. But I thought, no, I'll surprise the old uns. I took a hotel room in town, and left me motor-car there. I put on the old clothes I used to wear at the diggings, and I walked out here. I was going to knock on the door and pretend that I'd come back as poor as I'd left – but I had money in me pockets, and a gold nugget and a big opal. I was going to bring it all out and see the look on their faces.

' "I got here, and the cottage was even smaller and dirtier than I remembered. The thatch was going, and weeds was tall round the door, and the plaster on the walls was falling off. I felt guilty," says the ghost, "that the old uns had been struggling on without me all this time. I went and knocked on the door, and me mother come to it and – her didn't know me! Her looked right at me, and didn't know me at all.

' "So I says, 'Can I have a sit by the fire and a drink, please, Missis?' I thought I'd pretend to be a stranger for a bit, and see how long it took 'em to figure out who I was.

' "But they didn't know me. When I went off, I was a skinny lad, and when I come back I was a big, bearded man. They hadn't seen or heard me for nigh on twenty years – how would they know me?

' "They asked me in, and give me a cup of thin, poor ale, and a piece of bread spread with dripping. 'It's the best we have, I'm sorry,' says my old mother, and I felt worse. I was ashamed to say who I was. I sat talking with 'em, about how they managed, about how me mam was finding it hard to trail over the common after the goats when they slipped their tethers, and how me old dad was finding it harder to dig the vegetable patch and patch up the cottage. It was harder and harder for me to come out and tell 'em who I was. It felt like I'd be mocking 'em. So, since it was getting dark, I asked if I could stop the night.

' "I'll make you up a bed on the hearth," says me mam. And I laid me down afore the fire and went to sleep . . .

' "And never woke up again," says the ghost. "Not living. In the night, while I was sleeping, they come out, the old couple, me mam and dad, and they put a pillow over me face and smothered me, and they stabbed me again and again. They murdered me. And they took the money from me pockets, and the gold nugget and the opal. They must have heard the money chinking. They had such a longing for that money, for a bit of comfort, a bit of ease. They murdered me and took it."

'The vicar's wife says nothing. Her just sits a while, with

her hands folded on her Bible and her head bowed. Then her says, "Do you know where your bones are buried?"

' "I'll take you there," says the ghost. "And when my bones are buried in holy ground, and the prayers said to put me at rest, I'll haunt this place no more."

'So the vicar's wife got up, and her followed the ghost out of doors. The ghost had a kind of a shine about it that lit the darkness around it a little, and so her could pick her way. The ghost took her to one corner of the vegetable patch, and hovered there. The vicar's wife bent over and put her Bible on the ground, so her could find the spot again.

' "If your mam and dad are still living," her says, "they could hang for this."

' "Oh, let 'em be, let 'em be," says the ghost. "I was bringing the money to them, and they've got it. I hope it's brought 'em some happiness, for all they must have the sin on their minds. They're old and can't have much longer to live. I shall be at rest soon: leave them in peace an' all."

'So that was the way it was. The vicar's wife told her husband what had happened, and the vicar and the tinker dug up the vegetable patch and found bones there.

'The vicar buried 'em quietly in the churchyard; and the tinker's family lived quietly in the cottage. There was no more haunting.

'It was all supposed to be hushed up, but acourse, the story got out. Stories always do.'

'What about the old couple?' Clo asked. 'Did nothing happen to them?'

'The way I heard it,' Letty said, 'was that vicar wanted to go over and see the old couple, and tell 'em all about the ghost and how it was laid – "to give 'em a chance to square their consciences and make their peace with God," he said. But his wife said, "What use would that be? They must find it hard enough to sleep and say their prayers as it is. If they find out it was their own son they killed, why, they'll run mad. Leave 'em be, like the ghost said, and let 'em find their own way to heaven, if they can." Now that's a true story.'

All the food was ready and the table spread, but the funeral party wouldn't be back yet a while. The three women sat down with cups of tea.

'Haven't you got a story to tell us, Clo?' Letty asked.

Clo thought about it, and nodded. 'I can tell you one,' she said. 'And this one's true an' all. You know Sutton Chase?'

Oh, they knew it. A long, wide stretch of moorland and straggling forest, broken with streams and boulders, and crossed only by thin footpaths and two rutted cart-tracks. Over this wild land, long ago, the old kings chased the deer.

'You know how nobody wants to cross it on their own, or after dark,' Clo said.

Letty and Granny Shearing nodded. People had set off alone to cross the Chase, but had never reached the place they were going. They'd met with robbers and been murdered, or had lost themselves among the moorland hills and died, cold and alone. After dark, their ghosts wandered the Chase, crying, complaining, trying to lead living travellers to the same death.

'Well, there was a pedlar-lad,' said Clo. 'He'd been off on his rounds, with his pack on his back, going from farm to farm, and from village to village, selling needles, pins and thread, and buttons and ribbons and lace and laces and buckles. Most of his journey he'd been lucky. He'd found other people to travel with, or he'd always managed to come to a village or a farm well afore dark. But now he was on his way back home to the town, and his luck ran out. He didn't find nobody to travel with. He hung about in the village at the edge of the Chase, hoping somebody would come along and nobody did. He should have waited, even if it took days – but he wanted to get back to his lodgings in the town, where he could rest up for a bit. He'd been on the road for weeks. So he thought he'd chance it, and walk fast all the way, to make up for lost time. But he was still on the road when it fell dark. He knowed there wasn't a house for miles.

'He kept walking 'cos he hadn't any choice, and it kept getting darker, until he was tripping as he went, 'cos he couldn't see the ruts and hollows. Every sound he heard, he thought of ghosts or robbers – he kept thinking he heard footsteps and shouts or moans.

'Then a boulder at the side of the track stood up. Pedlar-boy near died then and there. He thought the ghosts had come to get him. Or the robbers.

' "You'm late on the road," says the boulder. It was a man who'd been sitting down on a smaller rock. He had a big dog with him, a big, slinking hound. Pedlar-lad still can't speak, he'd such a shock. "Don't worry about the dog," says the man. "He's big but he won't hurt you. You benighted?" The lad nods. "You'd be better under a roof," says the man. "You want somewhere to stop the night?"

'Pedlar-lad gets his voice back and he says, aye, he would, please.

' "Come and stop with we," says the man. "We live over the rise there. Come on."

'So the pedlar-lad leaves the track and goes with the man and the dog across the moor, through thorn bushes and up a steep hill. The man tells him he's one of the miners who lives on the Chase in out of the way places, digging for coal. They plod over the top of the hill, and then the pedlar can see a light shining through trees and bushes. "Go on down and knock at the door," says the man. "Tell 'em Joe sent you. I got a few things to do." And he goes off into the dark with his dog following him.

'The pedlar-lad goes on down the hill to the little house as well as he can in the dark. He trips and stumbles, and branches whip him across the face, but in the end he gets to a bit of cleared yard round the house. There's a window that's shining all bright with firelight, and it's nearer than the door, so he goes to it and looks in.

'Inside there's a little room with an earth floor and not much furniture. An old woman's stooping over and throwing dirt on the floor, like you do to soak up something that's been spilt. And at the back of the room there's two big men, and an open chest, and the two men have got something between 'em, and they'm bundling it into the chest.

'The pedlar-lad's glad to think he's going to be indoors in the warm soon, and he taps on the window, friendly-like. The woman and the men inside give a big jump and look up, all startled. The woman throws dirt about even quicker, and the two men shove the thing they'm holding into the chest and bang down the lid. Pedlar-lad feels a bit guilty, even a bit scared. He don't want to make these people angry.

'He goes to the door and knocks. One of the big men pulls it open and stands there glowering at him. "Joe told me to come!" says the pedlar-lad. "I was benighted on moor. Joe said I could stop here the night."

'Then the old woman and the other man come to the door, and the old woman pulls the lad in by the arm. "Poor lad," her says. "Come to the fire. I'll get you something to eat. Are you on your own, then?"

'Everybody's smiling at him now, and the lad feels happy to be safe with these people, and off the lonely road and out of the dark. He sits by the fire and tells the old woman and her two sons how he come to be travelling the road by hisself so late at night.

'The old woman give him a bowl of stew and some bread. "You was in a hurry to get back to your family," her says. "They must be missing you."

' "Oh, I ain't got any family to miss me," says the lad. "Me mam and dad am dead. Ain't got nobody else."

'The old woman and her sons slide their eyes to the side, to look at each other.

' "You'm a pedlar!" says the old woman. "Let's see what you've got in your pack then!"

' "Oh, I haven't got much left – just a few odds and ends," says the lad. "I've sold almost everything I had."

' "Good money, then?" says one of the two big sons, and their eyes slide to look at one another again.

' "Let me have a look in your pack anyroad," says the old woman, really friendly. "I never get to anywhere there's shops, so give me a look."

'So the pedlar-lad opens up his pack and spreads what he's got left on the floor. He's got his money in the pack, in a bag, and he snatches it up and puts it in his jacket, quick, and he don't think anybody's noticed.

'While the old woman's picking through his packets of needles and hanks of thread, Joe comes in, with the big hound. "This is a poor little waif and stray you've brought home," says the old woman. "He's all alone in the world."

' "He's done good business, though," says one of the sons. "He's got a good big bag of coin in his jacket. Haven't you?" And he slaps the lad on the back.

'The pedlar lad just laughs. He's starting to feel unhappy, but what can he do? It's pitch-dark outside by now. He's got nowhere else to go. So he tells hisself not to be daft, that he's lucky to be in a warm house with such friendly people.

'The old woman opens a door off the kitchen. "I'll put you to sleep in here," her says. "You must be tired out, poor lad.

You'll be wanting to get your head down and off to sleep."

'There's nothing in the room when the lad looks into it but a bed of rags and straw on the floor in one corner. "You can have it all to yourself," says the old woman. "Get a good sleep. Nobody to disturb you."

'The lad feels even worse at the thought of being in this room, on his own, in the dark. "Can I have a candle?" he says.

' "Of course you can have a candle, my love," says the old woman, and her gives him one.

'Even when he's got his candle, and he's curled up in the bed of rags, the lad has hard time getting to sleep. The candle leaves all the corners dark, and it's more like being in a dark cave than a house. But he's tired out, and he's just had a sit by a fire and a big bowl of hot stew after being out in the cold wind all day. He drops off to sleep.

'Something wakes him up. The candle's still burning on the floor by the bed of rags, so he can't have been asleep for long. He thinks it was a shout woke him. He looks round, at the close walls and the low ceiling and the dark shadows, and something moving catches his eye and makes him jump. Something's running under the door of his room from the kitchen. A long stream of something, running fast and spreading over his floor. Water? he thinks. Stew, spilled from the pot?

'He picks up the candle and crawls out of bed and over the floor to the stream under the door. In the candle-light, the stream shines red. He knows the smell. It's a stream of blood.

'He's nearly too scared to think or breathe, but he knows he's got to find out what's happening. He steps over the stream of blood and gets close up to the door – and it's an old, battered door made of planking, and there's lots of little cracks opened up between the planks, and one big knot-hole knocked right out. So he puts his eye to these cracks and this knot-hole and peers through into the kitchen. It's all shadows and firelight, and two of the big brothers are struggling with something in the middle of the room, and the stream of blood's running from whatever it is. The lad goes cold right through to the marrow of his bones and his hair moves on his head – but then one of the big brothers moves aside, and the lad sees a shaggy, hairy coat – and it's a goat. The thing the brothers am struggling with is a goat. They've just cut its gizzard.

'The lad nearly laughs out loud. Only a goat! He puts his hand on the latch of the door. He's going to go out into the kitchen and have a laugh with 'em all about how scared he was. Just as he's lifted the latch, one of the brothers says, "I wish all the throats we cut was as easy as a goat's."

'The old woman laughs, and her says, "Did you ever hear such a yelling and screaming as that old man give out of him?"

' "And then that lad comes knocking at the window just as we'm stuffing him in the chest!" says one of the brothers.

' "And there was I, spreading earth to soak up the blood!" says the old woman.

' "I thought I'd fill me pants!" says her son. And they all

115

laughed. When they stop laughing, the one called Joe says, "You going to kill the lad tonight, or wait till the morning?"

' "We'll clean the goat first," says one of the others. "Then we'll do the lad. It'll be easier while he's asleep."

'The lad holds his breath and lets the latch of the door down gently, so it don't make a noise. He turns round so fast, looking for a way out, that the candle flutters in his hand and nearly goes out. He holds still and the light steadies. At the back of the room there's one little shuttered window. It's not hard to push the shutters open and climb out, and the lad does it in a minute – but he has to leave his candle behind, and it's dark, and the ground rough with tree-roots and rocks and brambles underfoot. He tries to sneak away into the dark, but he can't see where he's going, and he loses his balance, and stumbles, and trips and falls and thrashes about in the scrub.

'The people in the house hear him. One of the brothers opens the door of the bedroom and looks in. "He's away!"

'Joe says to his big dog, "Seek! Seek!" And when the dog dances and wags its tail, he opens the door and lets it out. "Seek him! Fetch him!"

'Off into the dark goes the dog, coursing through the scrub and thorns. The dark didn't bother it – it had the lad's scent – and it could run faster than the lad.

'The poor lad hears it coming, and he sobs aloud, and runs for all he's worth, not caring if branches cut him across the face – bashes hisself against boulders and goes on for all the hurt – though he knows it's hopeless, and the dog'll catch him – and then he falls headlong, full pelt, and dashes hisself on a heap of rocks. He give his head a clout that nearly knocks him senseless, and the blood comes gushing out – and he gashes his hands and knees an' all, and they bleed.

'He's dazed and giddy for a second, but then he hears the rough gasping of the dog, and the rush of it coming through the scrub after him – and somehow or other he staggers to his feet and stumbles off again, with his head ringing and his knees weak under him.

'He hadn't a chance, not a chance – but the dog come on all the blood spilt on the rocks, and it stopped, and lapped up the blood, and when its masters come up, it was still there, wagging its tail, all pleased with itself. See, it thought it had caught up with the lad, cos it had found the blood. The men tried to set it on again, but it wouldn't follow that scent any more.

'The lad thought the dog was still after him, so he went stumbling and dragging on, all giddy and sick and weak. He didn't dare stop, for all he didn't know where he was going.

'The men hunted round for him – they didn't want him to get away and raise the alarm – but it was dark, and they was among scrub and thorns and forest and broken ground – and the lad found all the cunning of a mouse with a cat after it. He crept into hollows and ducked into thickets and by luck, by sheer luck—'

'By God's good guiding Hand,' said Granny Shearing.

'– he found his way again to the main track over the Chase. Now he knowed that what he had to fear was behind him, and he set off along that track as fast as he could go, though his cut knees and shins was sinking under him, and his head was reeling. When it started to get light, he didn't know if he felt more hope, or more fear that the men behind him would be able to see him – but he kept going, and it was full light when he reached the end of the Chase and come into a village. Up to the first house he went and banged on the door, and tried to shout, but couldn't do more than croak.

'When the woman of the house opened the door, her found the lad collapsed on her doorstep, in a terrible state, his face covered in blood and his clothes all blood-stained an' all. Her called her husband and, between 'em, they helped the lad in to the house and laid him on a bed.

'They called in other neighbours, who might know more what to do for him, and when the lad started to croak out what had happened to him, they fetched out others, and pretty soon half the village is crammed into this one little house. And then all the men got together and they went out onto the Chase, to visit the old woman and her three sons.

'They found the old woman at home, but the three sons had taken off. They knowed, see, that since the pedlar-lad had got away, folk would be coming for 'em. But they caught 'em, all of 'em, and took 'em away for trial.

'They dug up the ground round the old woman's cottage, and they found the bones of all the travellers they'd murdered over the years. And after that, four gibbets went up on the Chase, and the old woman and her three sons swung from 'em in chains until they was nothing but bones, and then until the bones fell apart.

'And now, if you go over the Chase after dark, it's them four you hear calling and whispering along the tracks after you; and you hear the howling of the dog, and its thumping paws racing after you, just like the pedlar lad heard 'em. And that's why folk won't go over the Chase after dark.

'What happened to the pedlar lad?' asked Granny Shearing.

'Oh, he got better, and he took to the road again, but he never again let hisself be benighted. He never travelled over the Chase alone again. He made sure he spent the night at some inn or farmhouse where he knowed the folk and could trust 'em.'

'Very wise,' said Letty, who was looking out of the window. 'Here they am, all coming back. Put the kettle on the fire. They'll be wanting a cup of tea.' Then her opened the door and called out, 'Was it a good funeral?'

Four

A New Baby

The bed had been brought down to the ground-floor room, and the mother lay in it, dozing, with the new-born baby sleeping beside her. On a chair beside the bed, watching over them both, sat Granny Shearing. Spread over her lap was a smock, and she worked at decorating the front with draw-work. Her sharp scissors snipped threads in the cloth, which she drew out, making a pattern of lacy holes.

In the kitchen Letty measured flour to make dumplings for a stew. She had to make enough for the new mother and father, and their older children, and have enough left over to carry home to her own family.

The door of the house stood open, and Clo sat on the doorstep with the new baby's brothers and sister, amusing them by weaving wool about her fingers in a cat's cradle.

'Tell we a proper story, Clo!'

'If you like. What story?'

'A long one.'

'Tell we one about a babby.'

'Hmmm.' Clo went on weaving wool about her fingers.

'I know one that's got a babby in it.'

'That one then!'

'Tell it.'

'Well then,' said Clo. 'Once upon a time – not your time nor my time, but a good time – Once on that time, when pigs were swine, and monkeys chewed tobacco – when cows and sheep went "Quack quack quack" and nothing seemed to matter – In that time, that good, good time, I took meself off over hills, dales and high, high fells. I walked and I walked, far, far further than I can tell you tonight, nor tomorrow night, nor any other night this five year. And I come to a place where the cocks never crew, the wind never blew, and never a single tear was shed – and in this far-off place I heard this story . . .

'So be quiet!

'Sit still!

'Listen!

'And remember.

'You little blood-wag bleed-oranges, two toots of a rag-man's trumpet, toot, toot!'

Giggling, the children shoved each other, and settled down on the trodden earth around the doorstep. As they listened, they picked sprigs of the lavender that grew there, in bushes and, squeezing the leaves, released the sharp scent.

'Once there was this wench, an ever-so-pretty wench, but oh! her was idle. As idle as her was tall, as idle as her was pretty. Her spent her time sitting in the sun and twisting her hair round her fingers. The only time her moved off her backside was when there was men or boys around to flirt with.

'Her mother was always on at her. "Afore you go traipsing off round the houses, there's spinning to be done," her'd say. Or, "Why don't you cook the dinner tonight and give me a chance to get on with something else?"

'And the wench'd say, "I don't want to." Or, "I'll do it another day, don't keep on."

'Then her mother'd lose her temper. "You might think a pretty face is all you need to get by in life," her'd say, "but you'll find out how wrong you am, my fine young madam. You can't knit, you can't sew, you can't brew or bake or spin; you don't know nothing about keeping house. Combing your hair and eyeing up the men ain't going to get you very far – or not to any place worth going, anyroad."

' "Oh shut that big hole in your face," says the wench. "You'm giving me earache."

'Then the mother got good and mad. "Why, you little baggage!" her says. "Answering me, you mouthy piece! You useless, flaunting bit of trash!" With every word, her gives her daughter a slap or a thump. The wench runs off, and her mother grabs her by the hair to pull her back, and both of 'em are screeching, and out into the road runs the wench, with her mother right behind her, pummelling her body.

'And it's just their luck that, as they run out into the road, along comes the young lord in his motor-car; and he sees this pretty wench being pulled by her hair and whacked and clouted. He pulls up and says, "Hey! Hey, have a care. Let be,

Mother. What's her done to deserve this?"

'The mother's all red faced and out of breath, with her hair falling down, and her's a bit put-out to find herself under the lord's eye, but her speaks up for herself. "What's her done? Nothing! Her never does nothing, that's her trouble! Bone-idle her is. Look at her! Look how big her is! And her can't spin worth a spit, can't cook, can't knit, can't do nothing!"

' "That's not fair!" says the wench, all in tears. "I CAN spin! I CAN! I can knit and spin better than anybody!"

' "Oh, telling such lies!" says her mother.

' "I'm not lying! I knit and spin better than anybody in six counties round!"

'Well, the young lord's looking at this pretty wench, standing there in tears, and truth to tell, he took a fancy to her. He thinks it's a shame that her has to live with this wicked old mother who beats her. "Are you really the best spinner and knitter in six counties?" he says.

' "I am, I am!" her says.

' "You know," he says, "my old housekeeper up at the castle's getting hard of sight, and her old fingers are stiff, and her can't manage the spinning and knitting any more. Her could do with a young wench to help her. Would you like to come and live at the castle and do my knitting and spinning?"

' "Oh, ar!" says the wench – 'cos her thinks it'll be grand to live at the castle, where her mother can't always be nagging at her – and then, the lord's a beautiful young man, and rich an' all. So the lord reaches over his seat and opens the back door of his car, and the wench gets in, and they drive off to the castle. There's the wench, sitting in the back of the motor-car, waving like a queen to everybody they pass, and thinking her's made for life.

'Well, they drives into the castle, and the lord's old house-keeper come to meet 'em. "This here's a wench I've brought to help you with the spinning and knitting," says the lord. He wouldn't let on that really he'd brought her home cos he fancied her. "Her's the best spinner and knitter in six counties round," he says.

'The housekeeper's glad to hear that. "We've whole load of fleeces in store that need carding and spinning and knitting up," her says. "You come along with me, my love. We'll soon find you something to do."

'And her takes the wench into one of the castle store-rooms that's full, floor to ceiling, of all these fleeces, and her says, "I'll leave you to be getting on with it." And off her goes.

'The wench's left there on her own, and her pulls out one of the fleeces and unfolds it, and looks at it, and then her throws it down. Puts her hands on her hips and stands looking at all the others. 'Cos her mother was telling the truth, and the wench can't card, or spin or knit worth a spit. Her hates doing it anyroad. It dawns on her that her ain't going to be able to get out of work so easy at the castle as her could at home. So her kicks the nearest fleece. "The devil fly away with it!" her says. "The devil can card and spin and knit it for all I care!"

'And then there's a man standing by her, who wasn't there

before. He's got a little pointed beard and a moustache, and he's wearing hat. There's long tails to his coat, and his boots have got broad, round toes. "In trouble, m'dear?" he says. "I'd like to help you. How about if I make sure that all these nasty old fleeces are washed and carded, and spun, and knitted?"

' "Oh, could you?" her says. And her twists her hair round her fingers and smiles and makes eyes at him. "Would you? I'd be ever so grateful."

' "No need, m'dear," says the man. "We'll make it a simple business proposition. I do the work, and you pay me."

'The wench goes all pouty. "I got no money," her says.

' "I'm not asking for money," he says.

' "What, then?" says the wench, and smiles and sways her hips, and looks up and down.

' "Your first-born child," he says.

'That stops her smiling – but her ain't got no children, nor any plans to have any. Her don't want none, come to that – dirty, squalling, pestiferous nuisances that they be. So her says, "Oh, ar, I agree to that. Come on then – spin me some thread to show 'em."

'The man in black catches up a fleece, shakes it, whirls it round his head – and then winds it up and hands her a big hank of spun thread, all neat and smooth.

'The wench takes it away and shows it to the housekeeper, who peers at it, and feels it with her fingers, and says, "That's the best spun yarn I've ever come across in the whole of my puff! And so quickly done too! Have it back and knit it up

125

into stockings, my love, and let's see if you're as good at knitting."

'The wench went back to the store-room, where her could be quiet and by herself, and her says, aloud, "I need this thread knitted up into stockings!" And the hank of thread twisted in her hand, and whirled about, and knotted and knitted itself, and fell down round her feet in a heap of stockings. Her gathered 'em all up and took 'em to the housekeeper, who couldn't get over how beautiful the knitting was. Her showed 'em to everybody.

'After that, the wench was given a room of her own to live and work in, with a fire to keep her warm, and a bed, and all the food and drink her wanted. Her used to take a couple of fleeces in there with her, and wish for 'em to be spun into thread and knitted up into jumpers, or dresses or shawls, or whatever, and then her used to sit combing her hair, and watching as the magic worked. Her never give a thought to the bargain her'd made. After all, her still didn't have no children.

'When her got bored with sitting in her room, her used to go off round the castle, down into the kitchens, out to the stables and the kennels, gossiping with everybody and flirting with all the men, as usual.

'There was an old hen-wife who had a little house inside the castle-walls, and who used to look after all the castle's poultry, feeding 'em and collecting the eggs. Some folk said her was rough under the foot – hairy on the bottom of her feet. That's the mark of somebody who can turn theirselves into a hare. A witch. That old hen-wife knowed a sight more than her prayers – and her was a great old gossip an' all. Knowed more of everybody's business than they did theirselves. So this old hen-wife and our wench got to be good friends. It didn't take the hen-wife long to twig that there was something funny going on. Her knowed that such fine knitting and spinning ain't done in a few minutes, leaving you all the time in the world for running round the castle, chatting and making eyes at everything in trousers. So the old hen-wife asks a few questions, and the wench told her everything, laughing and giggling at how clever her was being, fooling everybody. Her hadn't got no more sense. "But you won't tell nobody, will you?" her says to the hen-wife.

' "I shan't even tell me cat," says the hen-wife. "But what I want to know is, what are you giving our friend in black in return for all this knitting and spinning?"

' "Oh, just me first-born child," says the wench.

' "That's a steep price to pay," says hen-wife.

' "Oh, but, see, I ain't got any children," says the wench, and giggles again.

' "But you might have, one day," says hen-wife.

' "Oh, I'll worry about that when it happens," says the wench; and off her runs to find somebody else to talk to. The old hen-wife potters on about her chores, and does a lot of thinking.

'Now while the wench was running about the castle, laughing and talking with everybody, her often met the young lord, and her'd flirt with him, same as her did with all the other men. Her was so pretty, and always so lively and happy, that he was more and more taken with her. Fact, he fell in love with her. An' he knows what a good spinner and knitter her is. He thinks her must be a good cook and housekeeper an' all – well, her's so pretty! Her must be. And the end of it is, he asks her to marry him. Well, her ain't going to turn him down! Her sees a life of comfort and plenty stretching ahead of her.

'So the wench become the lady of the castle, and her was never happier. All the young lord asked her to do was to spin and knit, and her only had to ask, and the fleeces spun and knitted theirselves in a couple of eye-blinks. After that, her could what her liked – and what her liked was to put on a pretty frock, and a pretty hat, and take a drive out in the motor-car, winking and waving at every man her saw – or her'd gossip with the old hen-wife. The wench thought things'd go on like this for ever. Ah, but things always change. The wench found out her was going to have a babby.

'The first her knowed on it was when her wished for some fleeces to be spun and knitted up into long woollen dresses for all the maids in the castle – and there was the man in black, standing alongside her in his long-tailed coat and his broad-toed shoes, with his hat on his head. "Morning, m'dear," he says. "I shall soon be collecting my payment."

' "What payment?" her says, cos her'd all but forgot making any promise about payment.

' "Why, don't you know you're going to have a babby in

nine months' time?" he says. "And when you do, I shall come and fetch it away. In payment."

'Well, the wench wasn't too bothered. "What do I want with a babby anyroad?" her thought. "Nasty, noisy, messy thing, taking up all my time. Let him take it away and good riddance."

'But as the months went by, her started to think different. The babby growed inside her, and her started to think her'd like to have a good look at it afore the man in black took it away. And then her started to think that her'd like to have it around for a bit, just to see what it was like to be a mother.

'And what was the man in black going to do with the poor little thing anyroad? The more her wondered about it, the more her lost her smiles and chatter. Her drooped and dragged about the place. Couldn't be bothered to flirt any more. Couldn't be bothered to gossip. But her still used to go and see the old hen-wife.

'The hen-wife soon figured things out. "You'm going to have a babby, ain'tcha?" her said, and the wench nodded. "And you'm thinking about the bargain you made," says the hen-wife. The wench nodded again. "All you can do," says the hen-wife, "is beg for mercy next time you see *him*, and ask if he'll let you out of the deal."

'The wench thought it was worth a try. Her went straight to her room, and wished for some fleeces to be knitted up into breeches, and while the wool was whirling in the air, her says, "Let me see you – I need to talk to you."

'The man in black come out of the air, and stands with his arms folded.

' "I don't want to give you my babby," says the wench.

' "I'm sure you don't, m'dear," he says, "but I kept my side of the bargain. Now you must keep yours."

' "Take something else," says the wench. "Please!"

' "What else do you have that's yours to give?" he says.

' "Take my beauty!" her says, but he shakes his head. "Take my luck! Take ten years off my life." But he shakes his head again.

' "The only thing I want, and the only thing I will take," he says, "is your first-born child. As we agreed."

' "But I didn't know what it would mean!" says the wench, and her's crying.

' "I was plain enough," says the man in black. "I used no trickery. I told you clearly what I wanted, and you were happy to agree. You've had much in return. I shall have the one small thing I asked for in payment."

'The wench sat down on the floor in a heap, and her sobbed and cried, and begged and pleaded, and in the end the man in black laughed and said, "If you can tell me my name afore your child is born, I'll consider our bargain closed. But if you can't name me right – and you won't, you won't! – then I shall and I will have the child."

'The wench gets to her knees and says, "Is it John?" Her thought her'd better start guessing straight away.

' "No."

' "Harry?"

' "No."

' "Tom?"

' "No."

' "Dick?"

' "Three guesses only," says the man in black. "Three guesses every day. But if I give you three hundred, you'll never guess it." And he turned him round and disappeared.

'After that, the wench was as miserable as a wet cat. Her husband was worried, but he couldn't get out of her what was the matter – her was scared to tell him, 'cos of the lies her'd told about being able to knit and spin. Only the old hen-wife got to hear what was the matter.

' "Well, now there's hope," says the hen-wife. "Find the name and save the child."

' "But there's so many hundreds of names in the world," says the wench, "and it might be any of 'em. How am I to guess?"

' "Keep guessing," says the old hen-wife. "You might be lucky."

'So the wench asked everybody what their name was, and what the names was of everybody they knowed. Her wanted to learn all the names in the world. And when the man in black come next, her said, "Is your name Ives?"

' "No."

' "Is it Perran?"

' "No."

' "Botterel?"

' "Ha! No. And you'll never guess it."

'Day by day the babby went on growing inside her . . .

' "Is your name Bjorn?"

' "No."

' "Is it Alexis?"

' "No."

' "Is it Gianfranco?"

' "Nada!"

'Day by day the time of the birthing come closer . . .

' "Could your name be – Rumpelstiltskin?"

' "Be serious."

' "Moon-calf?"

' "Never."

' "Puck?"

' "Wrong again! And you'll never get it."

'Day by day went by, and the wench's time come. Her pains started. Her was having the babby. Her sent a messenger to fetch the hen-wife, and when the old woman come, the wench grabbed hold of her hand and says, "I haven't guessed his name! What shall I do? The babby'll be born and he'll come for it, and I've only got three more guesses!"

' "Never you worry," says the old hen-wife. "Let me have a look at you." And then her says, "I don't think this babby'll be here afore tomorrow morning, so your man in black won't be coming afore tomorrow midnight, will he? So we've plenty of time."

' "But I've only three guesses!" says the wench.

' "Just you get on with having this babby, and let me worry

about everything else," says the old hen-wife. "By the way, where's your husband, and what's he doing?"

'The midwife speaks up and says, "We didn't want him hanging around here, so he's gone hunting to take his mind off things."

' "And where's he gone hunting?" asks the hen-wife. "Over Sutton Chase? Right-o. I think he might put up a hare or two out there. Now listen to me, lovie," her says to the wench. "I don't think that husband of yours'll be getting back home until tomorrow. Babby'll be born by then. When he comes up to see it, you mind you listen well to any story he has to tell. Now, I'll be off."

' "Oh stay, please stay," says the wench.

' "I can't," says the old hen-wife. "I've got important things to do." And for all the wench's pleading, off her went. Her went down to the castle kitchens, and asked for a little barrel of their strongest ale. Said that the lady of the castle had told her her could have it. The kitchen folk knowed her was a friend of their lady's, and they knowed the old woman was a witch, so they give her the little barrel her asked for, and off her set, carrying it, towards Sutton Chase.

'The poor wench went labouring on in her room at the castle, all through that day and past midnight – and the babby was born in the early morning. A lovely little wench, all perfect, and it was washed and wrapped up and put into bed with its mother. Who couldn't sleep, for all her was so tired, but lay there worrying about the next night, when the man in black would come and give her one last chance to guess his name afore he took the babby. Now her had the babby in her arms, the wench couldn't bear the thought of giving it away to anybody, let alone the man in black.

'It was just getting light when the lord's dogs come home by theirselves, their hair all standing up on end and matted with mud, and their tongues hanging out and their eyes wild. The kennel-boys tried to round 'em up, and kennel 'em, but they was all shy and jumpy, and kept growling and setting their ears back and running away. Seeing what a state the hounds was in – which nobody could understand – everybody was worried about the lord.

'But the lord come home safe around mid-morning, though he was spattered from head to foot in mud, and his clothes was torn, and he looked tired out. First thing, though, he asked about his wife and the babby, and when he heard that he had a daughter and his wife was well, he found the strength to run up to her room.

'Well, first he had to make much of his wife, and count all his little daughter's fingers and toes, and there was a lot of kisses and hugs – but when that was all over, he says, "I had a strange day's hunting. I was out by Selly Oak when the hounds put up a fine big fat hare, and off we went after her. Down by Nut Hurst and Doe Bank we went, and nearly had her, oh, a score of times, but always her'd give a leap, or a twist, or her'd find it in her to sprint a bit faster, and always her got away. Her run us all over the Chase, through mud and thorns and streams, but her was such a fine big hare that even when it got dark, we went on after her. And then, by

Blackroot Pool, we lost the scent. The dogs was casting round when I seen a fire jump up and start to shine through the trees – and then all the hounds turn tail and run, run away and left me."

'The wench is lying in the bed, listening hard to all this, cos her remembers the old hen-wife saying her had to listen to whatever story her husband told.

"Well, I creeps down to the fire," says the lord, "to see what was going on. And when I peers out through the bushes, you know what I seen? Witches! Witches dancing and oolooing round the fire, men witches and women witches, all of 'em stripped to the skin.

' "I was scared to death, I don't mind telling you. I was scared to move. I just crouched there in the bushes and watched. And sitting in the fire, like it was a chair – or a throne – there was a man. Would you believe it? Sitting in the fire."

'The wench shook her head in disbelief.

' "And then one of the witches come forward and – I was flabbergasted – it was our old hen-wife. It was. I saw her face quite clear in the light of the fire. Folk always said her was rough under the foot. And her reaches up into the fire and hands a barrel to the man sitting in it.

' "Well, he starts drinking, and soon he jumps down out the fire and starts dancing with the rest of 'em, except he keeps stopping to drink from the barrel. And I can see that he's dressed all in black – he had a long-tailed black coat, and a long tail, and horns on his head, and hoofs on his feet."

'The wench give a bit of a start when her heard this, but all her said was, ' "What happened then?"

' "Well, this old fella in black," says the lord, "he got drunker and drunker, and he was jumping in and out of the fire, and over it and through it; and then he gets so drunk, he yells, 'Witches, my witches all, next time we meet I shall bring you a feast – a sweet tender roast of babby, acos her'll never guess, in a million years her'll never guess that my name is Storm Weather, Storm Weather, Storm Weather!" And all the witches shouted out, "Storm Weather, Storm Weather!" So – I dunno what come over me – I jumped up and yelled, "Good weather, good weather!" Then all the witches screeched and howled and come after me – but I run like a good 'un, like a hare meself, and I got away in the dark. What d'you think of that?"

'Well, the wench said her was amazed, and thought her babby had a brave dad, and her was glad he was safe – but now her was tired and needed to sleep. So the lord went off to change his muddy clothes and have something to eat. The wench snuggled down in her bed with her babby, and her did sleep, for hours – 'course now her felt her had a chance at least.

'It got dark, and the wench was all alone in her room, with a fire burning, and then midnight come, and so did the man in black. "Ah, there's me babby," he said, "all wrapped up for carrying away." And he reached for the little thing.

' "I've still got three guesses at your name," says the wench.

' "Have your three guesses, then," says the man in black, and laughs.

' "Is your name Lucifer?" says the wench.

' "The man in black looks a bit put out. "No," he says. "Wrong track entirely."

' "Is it Beelzebub?"

' "No, no, nothing like it!"

' "Is it . . . could it be . . . Storm Weather?"

'He clenched his fists, and took a turn up and down the room, chewing his lip. Then he says, "I shall welcome you and your babby to my fireside, never fear – but later, not sooner." And he vanished.

'The minute he went away, every bit of spinning and knitting that had come from his magic turned into ashes. And the young lord, he'd gone hunting hares again that night and was out on the Chase, when his breeches and his stockings and the coat on his back all turned to ashes and blowed away in the wind. He was left in nothing but his linen shirt, and he had to come home like that, with Netherton moon a-shining. But he thought it was the doing of the old hen-wife and neighbourhood witches, getting their own back on him for spying on their meeting. He didn't say nothing about it, nor do nothing, 'cos he was frightened they might do worse.

'Next time the wench was asked to turn a fleece into knitting, her said, "Oh, the witches have put a spell on me an' all. Not a thread can I spin, not a stitch can I knit since the night you saw 'em dancing round the fire." The lord believed her, 'cos he was happy with her. So her went on dressing in pretty frocks and pretty hats and driving round the village in the motor-car, with her babby in her arms. And her'd go and see her mother, and say, "I can't brew or bake, or spin or knit, but I've done well enough for meself, wouldn't you say?" And her old mother gritted her teeth to dust.

'Then the wench'd go off to visit the old hen-wife, and let her hold the babby on her knee. Her was a wise old bird, that hen-wife. Knowed a sight more than her prayers, I can tell you.

'Snip, snap, snout, that tale's told out.'

'Tell we another,' said the children.

'Me tongue needs a rest,' Clo said.

'I know a story about a babby,' Letty said, from the fire where she tipped chopped carrots into the stew-pot. The children left Clo and went to stand near her. 'You want to hear it?' she asked, looking at them over her shoulder.

'Yes, please Auntie Letty.'

'Listen then,' Letty said.

'You all know Milking Bank Lane – well, there was a haunted place. For years it was haunted. Folk walking there after dark would hear a babby crying. Sobbing and crying, the noise following 'em through the dark. Well, you don't like to hear a babby sobbing when it's alive and there's something you can do for the poor little mite. But when it's dead . . . And crying so heart-broken . . .

'What had happened was, there'd been a young girl, and her young man got her in the family way. Her didn't tell nobody. Her was frightened to. The young fella whose fault it was would dump her if he knowed, her was pretty sure of that; and her mam and dad would have been furious. So her left her frocks ungirdled, and let 'em hang baggy, and her got away with it. Nobody knowed her was that way. And when her time come, her went away by herself, went into the woods round by Milking Bank Lane. Her laid herself down under a thorn bush, and had her babby all by herself – and a sight of suffering, poor soul. And her was that scared, not knowing what to do, frightened what her mam and dad was going to say, that her took that babby, soon as it was born, and smothered it with her hands. Smothered the life out of it. And hid its body under the thorn bush, covered it with leaves. And got herself home somehow. Poor wench. Poor babby.

'If her killed the babby and hid its body,' one of the boys asked, 'how does anybody know about it, to tell the story?'

'Here's a sharp un,' said Letty. 'Because, Your Honour, the poor wench took ill the day after, and thought her was dying, and her told what her'd done. That's how we know about it. They hung her, poor soul, for murder; and they found what was left of the babby and buried it – but outside the churchyard, and without a name, cos it had never been baptised. So it couldn't be give a proper burial in the churchyard.

'And always, after that, there was a babby crying in them woods and up and down Milking Bank Lane. Folk used to go ever such a long way round not to have to hear it.

'But there was this drunken man. He was so drunk, he forgot about the ghost. He was only thinking of getting home by the shortest way. So he was walking down Milking Bank Lane, with the trees arching overhead and making the road dark, but with the moonlight spottling through the leaves. There was a smell of wet grass, and bluebells, and he was singing a bit to hisself, quite happy – when he hears the babby crying. It was coming through the wood to him – stopping and starting like a babby might, toddling and stumbling along.

'It give him a start, and made his heart beat lollopy-lollopy, and he started off down the lane, fast as he could. But then the drink makes him brave, and he thinks: Hang on. It's only a babby, even if it is a ghost.

'So he stood and waited while the sobbing and grizzling got near; and then he shouts out, "What you crying for, little un?"

'And out of the dark wood, in a little voice, comes the answer: "I ain't got no name!"

' "Well, does that matter so much?" says the man. "If I hadn't got no name, I should still be the same."

' "I ain't got no name," says the voice in the dark wood. "No name! I ain't got no name."

'And the man thinks, if he hadn't got no name, *would* he be the same? Would folk know him, would they think of him in the way that they do, if he was named something different, or if he hadn't got no name at all. And he thinks, maybe it's something to cry about after all. He shouts out, "If you be a

140

girl, I name you Joan; but if you be a boy, I names you John."

' "I got a name!" says the little voice. And off it goes dotting, into the wood.

"I got a name! I got a name!" Further and further off, till it can't be heard at all. "I got a name!"

'And after that, there was never no babby heard crying in Milking Bank Lane. Its ghost had been laid to rest. All it had needed was somebody with a bit of nerve, to ask the right question. If ever you meet a ghost, you should always speak up and ask it what it wants. Remember that.'

'It's a bit spooky, that story,' said the little girl, who sometimes had to walk near Milking Bank Lane. 'Has the babby really gone?'

'Hasn't been heard for years,' said Letty.

'That was too short,' said one of the boys. 'Tell a longer one.'

'Will our new babby die?'

'No,' said Letty. 'Her'll be well taken care of.'

'Come over here,' said Granny Shearing, seeing that Letty needed to get on with her chores. 'I know a long story about a babby that was well taken care of.'

The children went to her, where she sat by their mother's bed. They climbed on the bed, and they, and their mother, all listened to the story while the new baby slept.

'This woman that this story's about,' said Granny Shearing, 'lived out by Old Yells Farm, in that bend of the road by Wakeman's Wood. Her had six children living, and was well-knowed as a good midwife and nursemaid. If somebody

141

wanted a babby delivered, or children looking after, they'd get her to do it if they could.

'So when there was a knocking at her door one dark night, her wasn't surprised. Babby's come whenever they please, at all hours of the day and night. Folk was always coming to fetch her out, to help at some birth or another.

'Her opened the door and shone her lamp out into the dark, and there on her doorstep was a tall, handsome man, all dressed up in a green coat and a weskit embroidered with flowers, and a gold ring in his ear. "I need your services," he says.

' "Just let me fetch me shawl," her says, "and I'll be right with you, sir."

' "There's no hurry," he says, and comes into the house. "The babby's already safely born. But I want to put it out to nurse, and I was told you could do it, and do it well."

' "That I can," her says. Her last born was still at the breast, see, and her had plenty of milk for two. "But we shall need to talk about the nursing fee."

' "Oh, you'll be well paid, don't fear," he says, and from his pocket he takes a bag, and starts to count out money on the table. "This is for the first month." Well, the woman just nods. He's only counting out what her expects to get. He adds a bit more, and her's pleased. But then he goes on counting money out, and counting it out, and her jaw drops a bit, but her don't say nothing – her don't *want* him to stop. He adds more money and more, until there's twice as much, and over, as her'd expect to get for a month. The man looks up and sees the surprise on her face. "I promised you a good fee," he says. "Now get your shawl, and we'll be off to fetch the babby."

'He's got hoss waiting outside – a big, tall, black hoss, whose eyes have a red shine to 'em. Bells hung on its reins, and every time it shifted its head, the bells rung. The midwife was a bit scared on it, but the man told her there was no need. He mounts up, and gives her a hand to get up and sit pillion behind him.

'Off they went, and oh! that hoss was fast. With every stride the bells on its reins all rung together, and every time they rung, the hoss flew faster yet. The midwife clung tight to the man, and tried to see where they were going – but the night was dark and everything went by at such a whirl that they could have been going north, south, east and west all at once for all her knowed. Her was worried – they was going so fast that, at this rate, they'd be out of the world altogether before an hour was up! But with the wind rushing in her face and the bells ringing in her ears, her couldn't find the nerve to say a single word.

'When the hoss did slow down, it was to trot in through the gates of a great house – big stone pillars stood on either side, with carved dragons on the top of 'em. The hoss carried 'em up a long drive, to the door of a beautiful stone house, with many windows and many chimneys, and steps up to a great door. Servants was waiting to hold the head of the hoss, and another servant come forward to help the midwife down from its back. The man dismounted hisself, and leads the midwife in through the front door, while the servants took the hoss away.

'Inside was a pillared hall, all built of coloured stone and gilded and hung with tapestries; and they went into a little room as pretty as a jewel-box, where a table was spread with a feast. There was wines, and hot meat and cold meat; and syrups and possets, and cakes and dainties – things the midwife had never seen or tasted before. The man pulled out a chair for her, and sits down hisself. "You must be hungry," he says. "Make a good meal – and the servants shall pack some of everything for you to take home to your family."

'The midwife could hardly thank him – and her was too nervous to do more than pick at one or two of the prettier dainties – but her promised herself her'd take a load of the food back with her and make sure her got her share once her was home.

'Seeing that her'd eaten enough, the man rung a bell, and the door soon opened and in come some more servants, carrying a cradle all covered in white velvet. They put it down on the floor by the midwife, and her looked into it and seen a babby sleeping with its thumb in its mouth – the prettiest, most perfect little babby her'd seen in all her natural – and being a midwife, and having six of her own, her'd seen a few.

' "This is the child I wish you to nurse," says the man. "Will you take him?"

' "Oh, I will!" says the midwife, thinking that her'd look

after such a little darling for half the money her'd been given – but her didn't say that.

' "I wish you to raise the child as you would your own," says the man. "But there are some strict rules I wish you to keep. First, you are not to teach him the Lord's Prayer, nor any other Christian prayer, nor any Christian doctrine. Will you agree to that?"

' "Well," says the midwife, "I hope you won't mind me teaching him right from wrong?"

' "Right from wrong, if you will," says the man, "but no Christian teachings."

' "All right. I agree to that," her says.

' "Secondly, every day that he is with you, you will find food and drink left in your house for him. You are to see that he eats and drinks all of this, though at other times, he may eat what your family eats."

' "If you'll see that the food and drink are delivered every day," says the midwife, "I'll see that he eats and drinks it."

' "Good," says the man. "Thirdly, you are never to wash the child after sundown."

' "That's an odd rule," says the midwife, "but easy enough to keep. I can promise you that."

' "I can see we'll deal very well," says the man. "My last rule is this: every morning you'll find a ewer of water left on your table. You are to wash the child in this *every morning* – but no one else is to touch it, or taste it, or have even a tiny splash on their skin. And you yourself must never taste it, or let it touch your face, and after washing the child, you must wash your own hands in plain water. Can you remember that?"

'The midwife repeated it all over, to show that her understood.

' "And do you think you can keep that rule?" says the man.

'The midwife thought of the generous payment her was getting, and her says, "I can, I promise you I can."

"Then let's drink," says the man, pouring out glasses of red wine, "to our agreement."

'After that he called for a carriage, pulled by six big black hosses with red eyes, and helped the midwife into it with the beautiful little babby, and the servants handed in hampers packed with all the dainties from the table. And the coach went even faster than the one black hoss had, and the bells on the harnesses rung as loud as church bells.

'The coach brought the midwife back to her house, and soon as all the hampers, and the midwife, and the babby was all out of it, it went off so fast, it seemed to vanish. The midwife's husband and her children all come out of the house to help carry the things in, and when they seen all the food, and the cradle covered with white velvet, and how beautiful the babby boy inside was, they all said, "Where've you been?" And the midwife couldn't tell 'em. "To a beautiful big house," her said, "but I don't know where it was. I don't even know if it was in this world."

'Well, the midwife looked after this babby boy for years, and kept all her promises – well, nearly all of 'em. Her never took him to church, and never told him anything out of the

146

Bible, nor taught him any prayers – though her did teach him right from wrong, as her seen it.

'Every month, when her woke up, her'd find a big bag of money on her kitchen table; and there'd be a flask of drink and a basket of food as well, and her always saw to it that the boy ate up all this food and drank the flask dry.

'The boy growed bigger, a'course, and whenever he needed new clothes, or new shoes, there they was, lying on his bed in the morning, and they was always of the most beautiful cloth and make. So they should be, for he was the most beautiful child anybody ever seen.

'Every morning on the midwife's kitchen table there stood a silver ewer of water, and every morning, just as her'd promised, the midwife washed the boy in that water, and then washed her own hands in plain water from her well. Her saw to it that nobody else in the family tasted the water in the ewer, or got a drop of it on 'em. Her often thought about washing her own children in it, though, 'cos her nursling growed up so strong and lively, and was never mopish or sick. And it seemed to her that he got stronger and healthier and more beautiful day by day, and that maybe the water had something to do with it.

'But then her'd think: If I break me promise, the money'll stop coming in – and the money helped her to feed her own children and to clothe 'em. And maybe, her thought, if the water's so magic, it'll do some harm to ordinary, mortal children – because her had more than half a thought, in the back of her head, that her nursling was something more – or something less – than a mortal child. So even though her was tempted, and tempted bad, her kept her promises. And the money, and the food, and the water kept appearing in the house – even though there wasn't hide nor hair to be seen of the nursling's father.

'Well, the nursling child growed up to be – well, I suppose he was about eight years old. He was small for his age, but very strong, and he could run and jump and climb better than boys twice his size. And he was a devil, into everything. He'd torment the life out of anything, whether it was chickens in the yard, sheep in the fields, dogs and cats, or other children. He'd bring the midwife home bunches of flowers he'd picked from other folks' gardens. He'd scrump apples and dam streams to flood paths, and throw stones at windows. And folk said he was a bit gone in the head, 'cos if he didn't have nobody else to play with, he'd play by hisself, and he'd run round, and hit out, and shout, just as if he *was* playing with somebody – but nobody was there.

'Folk forgive him, though – however mad they might be at first, they always forgive him in the end, 'cause he was so beautiful. His skin seemed to shine, and his hair shone, and his eyes was clear and bright like glass. His teeth white like milk. He was just a lovely thing to look at. It was the water from the silver ewer that made him so beautiful, the midwife was more and more sure on it.

'But still her kept her promise about the water – until a pedlar come to the door, selling this and that, and showed her some mirrors he had in his pack. Her looked into a mirror, and seen herself. Her hadn't really looked at herself for years. Now her seen all the lines round her eyes and her mouth, and the grey in her hair, and her couldn't rest after that. Every time her washed the boy in the water from the silver ewer, her kept thinking about what it might do for her. Would it wash away the wrinkles? If her wet her hair with it, would it take away the grey?

'In the end, her couldn't help herself. As soon as her nursling had run off to play after his wash, her rubbed the water all over her face and hair; and didn't wash it away with plain water either.

'Her couldn't see that it made her younger or more beautiful but, her thought, it might take more than one wash. So her went on washing herself in the water, day after day, feeling scared and guilty, but doing it all the same.

'Then, one day, the boy was having one of his mad half-hours, running about in the yard, playing with nobody and shouting to nobody, when the midwife looked out to laugh at him – and her seen that he wasn't on his own, after all. Her seen what her'd never seen afore – that he was running about and playing with half a dozen strangers – and strangers don't come no stranger than these characters. Some of 'em was shorter than the boy hisself, with noses a foot long. Some of 'em was seven feet tall and thin as a piece of string. Some was ugly, some was handsome, and the midwife knowed that only her and the boy could see 'em.

'Her said nothing to the boy, nor to nobody else. Folk'd

say her was mad an' all, if her said anything. Or else they'd say her and the boy was witches, and that could turn nasty. So her kept it to herself. And her didn't wash her face in the water from the silver ewer any more, either. But her went on seeing these other people, the ones that nobody else could see. They'd walk in through the door of her house and out again, just visiting and keeping an eye on things. Her'd see her nursling boy looking at 'em and smiling at 'em, but none of her own children seen 'em. They never looked at her or spoke to her, these things. They didn't know her could see 'em.

'Sometimes her'd find one sitting on the end of the boy's bed when her went to tuck him in. Her'd often catch sight of him walking and talking with 'em, or playing with 'em. After a while, her stopped worrying about 'em. They was no more to her than trees – and when you stop and think about it, trees am very strange things.

'It all went on like this until the day the midwife was at market, and her seen her nursling boy's father. He was dressed very fine, in his green coat, and he was going from stall to stall, picking up things he wanted and putting 'em in his pockets. Nobody took any notice. Well, nobody else could see him.

'Anyroad, he come towards the midwife. And her stood in his way and says, "Long time, no see! How are you these days? Your little boy's doing very well."

'The man stopped short and stared at her. "Do you see me?" he says.

' "I see you large as life – helping yourself to other folkses' livelihood," her said.

' "How do you see me?" he says.

' "With these two eyes," her says.

'And he raised his two fingers and jabbed 'em, hard, into her eyes. "Then see no more," he says.

'Her was blinded. Her put her hands to her eyes and cried out, and started feeling all round. Folk come to help her, and they peered at her eyes, and bathed 'em, and took her away to lie down in a dark room – but it was no good. Her was stone blind.

'Some kind soul took her home the next day, leading her all the way by the arm – and her husband and children all come running out, worried and scared. They didn't know what was going on, what with the midwife being away all night, and the nursling boy vanishing.

' "He's gone," they all said. "Just gone."

'They never seen him again and they never found out what happened to him. The money was never left on the table any more, nor the food and drink, nor the silver ewer of water.

'The poor midwife, her never saw her husband's face again, nor her children's, nor her grandchildren's. Never saw so much as twinkling of light till the end of her long life. Well, her should have knowed better than to break her promise to the man in green.

'You can break promises to plain ordinary folk and get away with it – but you'd better not break promises made to

151

Them. Better not to have owt to do with 'Em at all.

'But then, her'd have missed some grand sights, wouldn't her, if her'd turned the man in green away?'

Only the mother, dozing in the bed with her new baby, was still listening. The children, grown bored with such long stories, had run away.

THE STORY COLLECTOR

Susan Price

'Elsie, do you know any other stories?'
'Stories, Master?'
'Yes, you were telling one the other day in the kitchen, about a woman and the Devil.'
Elsie, with a thrill, sat down on one of the big polished chairs.
Mr Grimsby sat back in his chair and lifted his glass.
'Do begin.'
'Well, Master, it was like this . . .' Elsie said.

And so the Story Collector gathers his stories, from housemaids and soldiers, from dogs and the dying – tales of all kinds and about all things. There's a tale of a dancing shilling, a soldier who died too soon, three husbands humiliated, a stingy old man, a king subdued and a dog who told lies . . .

ORDER FORM

Susan Price

0 340 71031 4	THE BONE-DOG	£3.99	❑
0 340 62655 0	HAUNTINGS	£3.99	❑
0 340 65605 0	NIGHTCOMERS	£3.99	❑
0 340 70902 2	THE STORY COLLECTOR	£3.99	❑

All Hodder Children's books are available at your local bookshop, or can be ordered direct from the publisher. Just tick the titles you would like and complete the details below. Prices and availability are subject to change without prior notice.

Please enclose a cheque or postal order made payable to *Bookpoint Ltd*, and send to: Hodder Children's Books, 39 Milton Park, Abingdon, OXON OX14 4TD, UK.
Email Address: orders@bookpoint.co.uk

If you would prefer to pay by credit card, our call centre team would be delighted to take your order by telephone. Our direct line *01235 400414* (lines open 9.00 am–6.00 pm Monday to Saturday, 24 hour message answering service). Alternatively you can send a fax on *01235 400454*.

TITLE	FIRST NAME		SURNAME
ADDRESS			
DAYTIME TEL:		POST CODE	

If you would prefer to pay by credit card, please complete:
Please debit my Visa/Access/Diner's Card/American Express (delete as applicable) card no:

Signature ....

Expiry Date: ....

If you would NOT like to receive further information on our products please tick the box. ❑